THE PACK'S MATE

THE WOODLAND WOLF PACKS BOOK 1

AMELIA SHAW

DEXTER

My pack community grounds looked nothing like they did when I was a child. The once soft grass, still so fresh in my memory, was gone, worn down to dirt. The area, central to our town, was littered with beer bottles and cigarette butts, the playground equipment long since hauled off somewhere, probably to rot or rust in the woods. Out of our sight.

The sun was only just rising, but we were all up as usual, ready to start another long day's work. The heavy scent of testosterone filled in the air. My all-male pack, consisting of Taylor and Jay, bonded with the men with whom we grew up. Every one of them had been placed into small all-male families of their own now.

A sigh rippled through my throat as I glanced from the rock-strewn dirt at my feet, up to the pack. The group of men before me was a powerful, yet depressing sight. I loved these men. They were family, but I'd grown so tired of the same, familiar, *male* faces, day in, and day out. For a whole generation now, the Woodlands pack had not borne a single female.

Not one.

For almost sixty years, the elders of my pack had questioned what happened to our breed, but they had not been forthcoming with any answers, so far. What would happen to our genetic lines if there were no female mates to carry our children for future generations? No one could answer that, either.

My mother and her sisters were some of the last pack-born women, and all of them had produced at least three sons each.

Which would have been great if there had been some other pack females around to mate with, when we all came of age. But there were none.

What went wrong? No one knew.

What we did know was that there would be no more children born to our purebred wolf-shifting women.

It would be impossible. The last of our fertile females matured past breeding age almost twenty years ago, so there was no longer any hope of a savior being born for our pack.

Something had to be done. If we didn't find women to breed with soon, our pack would likely become extinct.

There was an obvious option, and that was something we had been putting off as long as possible, because we didn't really know if it would work. We had decided to bring human women into the pack.

We needed to venture into the cities and acquire human females for breeding.

But no one knew if that would actually work, as it had never been attempted before. And that's why we had waited so long.

We had waited *too* long. It was time to take action, before there was no pack left at all.

We had something called a fated mate in our world. Wolf shifters in my pack only bred with their true mate, the one chosen for them by Fate. We had no idea if a wolf shifter *could* mate with a human, in the sense of being a true fated mate pairing. It seemed unlikely, but with no wolf shifter females left, we had to try something to save our blood line.

I was told that if I ever met my fated mate, I would recognize her by her scent. There would be an instant attraction, an undeniable bond from the moment we laid eyes on each other. And when we touched... sparks would ignite. I didn't actually *know* if any of that was true or not, as I'd never experienced it before. No one my age had.

We had to rely on the stories our parents told us, which seemed to change with time, like fairy tales.

It was hard to know what to believe and what to discount; tough to discern between all the blurred lines between fact and fiction that had grown over the years. And if there were no more wolf-born women, did the fated mate concept still even exist? Would that magical, instant bond still exist outside of the pack community?

Probably not.

We were in uncharted territory and no one in the pack knew the answers, not even the elders. And everyone was afraid of what would become of us if the fated mate bond failed us all.

"Dex!" The greeting came out of nowhere, interrupting my maudlin thoughts. "Come quickly. It's your dad." Taylor, my Beta, came running at me at break-neck speed and grabbed my arm.

My dad?

"Where is he? What's happened?"

"Come on." Taylor tugged at my arm, then turned and ran in the direction of my parents' home. I followed behind, running to catch up and not thinking twice.

My father had been feeling unwell for months, and as one of the elders in our pack, that was a bad omen for everyone.

The elders are meant to be the strongest of us.

He can't die. Not yet. Not until we've secured the continuation of our bloodline.

Thoughts tumbled through my head, on a loop.

I'll be lost without him.

No. It's not his time to go. It can't be.

Taylor led me straight to my parents' house and into the lounge, where my father was laying on the couch and my mother was on the floor beside the couch, kneeling over him.

Dad's face was deathly pale and his breath wheezed in and out of his chest like it was consuming all of his energy just to stay alive for a few minutes longer.

He hadn't looked like that when I saw him last. "What happened?" I asked as I crouched down next to my mother. Fear scudded through my chest.

Mom turned and squeezed my hand. "Please, Dexter, please. Take him to the hospital in Little Creek."

Little Creek was the nearest human town. "Mom, no. You know that's not our way." Surely there was some other way to help him?

We had a healer in our pack, but he was rarely required for anything other than fighting injuries. Our paranormal genetics meant that we healed extremely fast and rarely fell ill, unless it was something very serious.

My mom grabbed my shoulders with surprising force. "Dexter, I am not ready to lose him. Not yet. He can't die. I am asking you to help your father. Take him to a doctor at the hospital. Please."

I looked at my father, who met my gaze with his own. He didn't nod, but he didn't shake his head no, either. Pain laced his expression and my heart jolted hard when, for the first time ever, I saw fear in my father's eyes. He didn't want to die.

The decision was made for me. I had to take him in.

"Right, let's do this. Taylor, grab Jay and the truck. Bring it 'round the front. I'll carry Dad out."

Taylor looked at me for a long moment, as though questioning my logic. But in the end, he saw that I was serious, and followed my instructions as any good Beta would.

"Thank you, Dexter! Thank you," my mother said, as she jumped to her feet and moved out of the way.

I leaned down and lifted my father up into my arms, grunting with the effort. He weighed more than me, and when he flopped against my chest I realized how weak he really was.

Up until yesterday, he'd been feeling unwell, but that was the extent of it. Mostly, he was still as strong as ever. Or so I'd thought.

Perhaps he'd been hiding this illness—or disease, or whatever was ravaging him—far better than I'd guessed.

I shifted him a little, arranging his arm over my shoulder and securing him properly in my hold so that I could safely carry him out to the truck.

"Let's go, Dad."

I didn't know if a human hospital could save him. I was suddenly concerned nothing could save him. I'd been blind to the seriousness of his condition, whatever it was. But if there was a chance to save him at the hospital, then we had to try.

I limped outside under the weight of my father's bulk, his ragged breathing echoing in my ear. His skin was clammy beneath my palms.

"Are you sure this is what you want, Dad?" I asked, as the vehicle pulled up.

If my father didn't want the humans to help him, then I wouldn't force him.

My father nodded, but just barely.

Okay. I was doing the right thing.

"Let's go then, old man."

That got the briefest of smiles from my dad as I hefted him as carefully as I could into the back seat of the full-sized truck.

Taylor helped me get him situated, then I climbed into the driver's seat.

I adjusted the rear vision mirror so I could see my father's ashen face during the drive.

"Little River is an hour away, so don't you dare die on us before I get you there, Dad."

I gave my words a threatening growl for good measure, and there was a weak laugh from the back seat. My dad couldn't muster any words, but he was still trying for humor.

Jay slid onto the floor behind my seat, at my father's feet, the perfect Omega. Lucky, we had good-sized trucks instead of small cars, or he would never have fit.

My pack was in, and my father wasn't getting any better just sitting here.

"Let's go."

I planted my foot on the accelerator and we took off toward the nearest town. I drove the roads as fast yet as safely as possible, my heart thundering in my chest the closer we got to Little River.

"Let's hope the human stories of hatred toward our kind have been exaggerated, huh?" Taylor joked, trying to ease some of the tension in the truck.

The silence had become overwhelming.

I managed to smile, though I suspected it might look more like a grimace. "Yeah, I think as long as none of us go shifting in the middle of the city, we'll be fine."

All of us of mating age had ventured into the cities for clandestine sexual encounters with random strangers on occasion, but we never went anywhere near the heart of the city, nor did we linger once our needs were sated.

We also steered clear of the hospitals and doctors when we were injured, in fear of the possibility of having our blood tested and finding a difference that they could not explain.

We'd been told since we were kids how much humans hated us. That they feared anything different and if they identified who—or in their eyes, *what*—we were, we'd be locked up in a zoo, or dissected on a scientist's table.

That was one of the reasons I didn't want to take Dad here to the hospital. Presumably they would need to take and test some of his blood. When it came back different to human blood...

I shook my head, figuring we would deal with that later. First priority was to get Dad well.

Taylor grinned and answered my earlier comment about shifting. "Yeah, I hope so."

We drove the rest of the hour in silence, broken only by the creepy rasp of my father's breathing.

Taylor pulled out his cell phone and directed me to the hospital using the maps feature.

"Turn left here. And it should be on our right."

The hair on my arms stood on end as we passed through the human city. So much light, so many people. A thousand shops and cars. Noise everywhere. Too much of everything. Chaos and cacophony that we weren't accustomed to.

My senses were already reeling when I pulled up outside the emergency department next to a hospital that stood a hundred feet tall.

"I'll take Dad in. Taylor, you park the truck and meet me inside. Jay, help me if you can."

Jay nodded and easily slid out the door, his agile, lithe body making every movement smooth and effortless.

I jumped out, opened the rear door and reached into the back seat for my father's form. His wheezing was getting worse. He was really struggling to breathe now, and his lips were turning blue.

His gaze on me was now full of fear, and I knew we couldn't waste any time.

I pulled my dad along the seat, hard. Adrenaline pumped through my bloodstream, making my muscles bulge and tingle with strength.

My instincts were telling me that Dad's time was almost up.

Jay got under my father's other arm and together we carried him toward the sliding doors.

They *whooshed* open and two men rushed out.

"Do you need help?" they asked, the foreign human scent rolling off their bodies making my hackles rise.

I grabbed for my father's huge bulk, a growl ripping through my throat as they attempted to take him from me.

Taylor pushed at me. "Dexter, they want to help. Let him go."

Fighting back the red shifting haze was harder than I thought.

I had to calm down, and fast.

Focus on Dad. Why you're here.

I gulped air into my lungs and forced my arms to unhook their death-like grip.

"This is my father. He can't breathe... I think it's his heart. Or his lungs. I don't know exactly, but his lips are blue."

"We need a gurney out here!" one of the men yelled and another man in uniform came running up pushing a white bed on wheels.

The man who'd called for the gurney touched my arm. "It's okay. We're going to take care of him."

"Thanks," I managed in a rough voice. They did seem like they were trying to do the right thing by my father.

2

DEXTER

I helped them put Dad on the bed and they wheeled him away quickly. His skin was gray and sweaty, his eyes were closed, and he didn't seem to be moving. Just in the hour trip between home and here, he had deteriorated substantially.

"What the hell is wrong with him?" I muttered to Jay. "And what are they going to do to him?" Jay squeezed my arm, hard.

"Let's follow them and find out."

I walked into a human hospital for the first time ever. I'd spent my life in the woods, fighting bear shifters and protecting my pack, and this truly was the strangest scene I'd ever witnessed.

The fluorescent lights burnt my eyes and the stark, white walls stretched up before me like an enormous maze.

I skidded to a halt before an indoor cage. The sign said reception desk, but it was a cage nonetheless.

The smell of sickness was almost overwhelming. It permeated my nostrils and I felt like I needed a long run in the forest to get the stench of illness out of my nose.

How did humans live and work in places like this?

A woman approached us and I searched my instincts. Despite the fact I hadn't seen a human woman in months, this one did nothing for me.

Her face was too coarse and pinched. Her aura was wrong and not attractive to me.

"Can I get you to fill in some forms for the man they just brought in? You're his son, right?"

I nodded, and she handed me a black clipboard and a pen. I managed to relax enough to sit on an uncomfortable plastic chair with Jay at my side.

Taylor came running in the door, spotted us and took the seat on my right.

The three of us against the world, as it had always been.

Pack mates. Alpha, Beta and Omega. Brothers, not by blood, but by a bond stronger than any other I'd shared.

"Whoa, I'd forgotten how hot these women are." Taylor whistled as more nurses moved about and patients staggered into the Emergency Room.

I shrugged my shoulders and focused on the human forms. "You're welcome to them, Taylor."

The pack took turns traveling to town, hitting up the bars. Finding women to bed for the night. I'd always struggled with fucking women I wasn't connected to. Slaking my lust and keeping my passions under control so I didn't hurt the fragile human women was not how I was designed.

The Alpha wolf inside me craved the constant contact of my true mate. A woman to love and protect. Someone to complete me and bear my children.

"What's wrong with you, Dex?" Taylor said.

I nearly answered, *my dad might be dying,* but that would have been churlish. I knew that wasn't what Taylor meant. I shrugged, looking at the various women in the room, before dismissing them.

Taylor frowned. "It's been months since we came to town. You must be horny as hell."

I was. But I'd been running miles every day to keep the horny demons at bay.

"I am," I admitted. "But I don't want any of those."

I gestured to the room as a whole and glanced up again as a young blonde woman stumbled over her feet as she stared at the three of us.

I didn't have any false modesty. I knew that we wolf shifters were appealing to human women. Our physical strength and good health were all out there for the world to see, and those I had hooked up with in the past had made it clear they would be happy for round two —or more—if I wanted it.

I'd just never wanted it that much.

I rolled my eyes and kept focusing on the paperwork. "When my mate shows up, let me know."

Jay sighed. "We may not have mates, Dex. A mate is a wolf shifter, pack-born. You know that's not our path."

I looked over at my Omega, battling to keep my sudden anger at bay, my gut burning at his words. "What is our path then? To die without a mate, lonely and childless? To watch the pack wither and die?"

Jay's mouth set in the grim line he always adopted when upset. "We're still a family, Dexter. Even without fated mates."

"I know that." I looked away, unable to properly express how I felt.

A lot of the men in our pack were content enough with their situation, but I wasn't. We'd grown up as one, huge pack, and at adulthood—twenty-one—we were ranked and chose who would share our own mini-pack of three.

I was ranked an Alpha, of course. All three of my brothers were Alphas, the same as my father.

As an Alpha, I was able to choose a Beta and an Omega to complete my family, my pack.

I was lucky. It was an easy choice.

Jay and Taylor had been my best friends from childhood and it was perfectly natural when we built a house and moved in together.

Our mini-pack, all ready for our mates.

But our mates didn't arrive, and despite how much I loved the guys, we weren't complete. There was a massive hole missing in my heart, and my life, and even if the other men didn't feel it as much as I did, it was still there, so prominent I couldn't deny it.

The receptionist returned to claim the clipboard full of information, and then we were left for what felt like hours.

"What's taking so long?" Taylor asked at one point, as he restlessly shifted on his chair, stood up, and began pacing back and forth around the seats.

We took turns wearing out the floor in the waiting area. There was nothing else to do.

I leaned forward on the chair and watched the white swinging doors that my father had disappeared behind. Over and over, they opened and closed.

And no one I knew walked through.

But eventually the doors did open, and a woman walked through. One I hadn't seen before.

I sat up straighter, my shifter instantly rising to the surface.

Who was she? And why did I suddenly want to take her in my arms and kiss the life out of her?

She was obviously a physician, dressed in blue scrubs and wearing running shoes that were well worn.

She spoke to the nurse, who pointed our way, and then the woman nodded and began to head toward us.

I jumped to my feet. My heart was pounding like I'd run a marathon, and my skin itched and vibrated like my wolf was about to spring forth.

"Dexter Monaghan?" she asked, meeting my gaze for the first time.

Sapphire blue eyes clashed with mine and a growl rolled through my chest. I only just managed to suppress the sound.

"Are you all right?" she asked, narrowing her eyes at my reaction.

Jay gasped and Taylor went rigid beside me. I could feel them reacting to her in the same way my shifter was, which should have been impossible.

We were meant to have our own mates. And she was *mine*.

I knew it with every fiber of my being.

I turned to my pack mates. "Go, wait in the car. I'll be out as soon as I can."

Jay's eyes narrowed, but he nodded and began to back away. Taylor set his jaw and shook his head. "No. I..."

I dropped my gaze away from my mate and turned to stare at Jay, willing him to do my bidding.

As the Alpha, my will was law, but I rarely exercised it with Jay or Taylor. I didn't want blind obedience from them. I believed that bred insolence and disrespect.

I wanted loyalty. Love. And trust. And those things were earned over time.

"Taylor. Go."

He turned and fled as the power reverberated in my command, and then I turned my attention back to the woman before me.

"Doctor...?"

"I'm Doctor Claire Masterson. I'm the physician treating your father."

"Claire..." I managed to say her name, even though all I wanted to do was put her over my shoulder and throw her into the back of our truck.

She looked at me strangely again, before lifting a hand and rubbing her arm in an absent manner. Was I making her nervous? I obviously wasn't behaving normally, and I didn't want to scare her off. But how to behave normally, when all I wanted to do... I shut down thoughts of what I wanted to do with this woman, and cleared my throat.

"I'm sorry, Doctor. Please continue."

She straightened, her throat working up and down as she swallowed hard. The woman looked almost as uncomfortable as I was. Perhaps she felt this strange electric connection, too?

"Your father had a massive heart attack," she began, and my own heart began to thump hard. *A heart attack?* Even with our shifter healing abilities, damage to the heart was not something easily fixed.

I blinked a few times, trying to concentrate on her next words. "A cardiologist has been paged, and I believe the plan is to operate tonight, inserting stents into his abdominal aorta. I'm here to give you an update and to let you know that there is a good chance of him surviving both the initial attack, and the surgery."

Thank you, God.

Relief winged through me with such intensity, it robbed me of breath for a moment. It was all I could do not to collapse into the plastic chair behind me, but I somehow managed to remain standing.

I'd talked myself into thinking there was no way my father could die today, but from the look of this woman's face, it had been a very real possibility. Likely still was, if the stents didn't work.

My mother had said she couldn't live without my father, and hopefully she wouldn't have to face that situation. Not for another three or four decades at least.

"How long until he can come home?"

She cocked her head to the side. "Let's take this one day at a time."

I ignored her human pragmatism. She didn't understand what my father was, nor what his healing capacities were.

"We live an hour away. I need to get my mother in to see him. If you could give me a rough estimate, I can let her know."

Claire hugged the clip board to her chest. "Best case scenario, he may be home within two weeks. But he'll need to be managed by a local doctor after that."

She didn't know that my dad's shifter genes would heal him post-operation, if the doctors could repair the damage to his heart.

"Thank you, Doctor."

I extended my hand to shake hers, my arm trembling with anticipation of her touch. According to the old stories passed down by my parents and pack elders, I would know my mate fully, the moment I touched her.

Claire reached over and took my hand.

Her gasp was as loud as mine, the electricity pulsing between us like a thunderstorm on a dark night.

It would have taken out my knees if I wasn't so determined to stand.

Claire wasn't so lucky. Her eyes rolled back in her head and she began to crumple to the ground. I stepped forward and swept her up into my arms before she hit the floor.

Her eyes fluttered as she struggled to stay awake. She stared up at me with a confused expression, her eyelids dropping to half-mast. "What happened?"

"The mating call."

Her eyes closed and her body went limp in my arms.

I glanced around. No one was looking in our direction, and no one seemed to have noticed what had happened yet with Claire. There was plenty of activity, including some kind of medical emergency near those white swinging doors, and everyone's attention seemed focused over there. The medical professionals all seemed to be concentrating on the task at hand and not the room at large.

I turned slowly and began walking toward the hospital exit doors.

"Excuse me!" Right as I reached the exit, I heard a woman call out behind me but I kept walking, forcing my legs to keep moving, even though the scent of Claire made me want to kneel on the ground and thank the Fates for sending her to me.

I couldn't stop or they'd take her away from me. I couldn't have that. My shifter would not allow it.

When I got out into the fresh air it was easier to breathe and I took a huge lungful. My head cleared and I began to wonder what I was doing.

"Dexter!" Taylor called out from about ten feet away, having pulled the truck up near the entrance.

I didn't think about it again. I went straight for the truck with Claire still prone in my arms.

"Hey!" There were noises indicating a commotion behind me and I was pretty sure Claire's absence from the hospital had finally been noticed.

Taylor opened the back door without asking a question and I put her into the back seat.

"Let's go!" I jumped into the back with her and held her tightly against me.

Taylor slammed the door, jumped into the driver seat, turned on the engine and gunned it out of the parking lot.

I looked down at the sleeping doctor in my arms. A human, and my mate.

And I had just snatched her from her human workplace, where my father was about to have surgery to save his life.

What the hell had I just done?

3

TAYLOR

"What have you done, Dexter?" I yelled over the revs of the engine as we sped away from the hospital like the devil was on our tail.

I could see them in the rear vision mirror—a group of security guards and nurses staring after us and pointing, as we kidnapped one of their doctors.

"I don't know."

Jay gaped at him from the passenger seat beside me. "What do you mean you don't know? What are we meant to do now?"

"Just drive, Taylor," Dexter grunted at me.

My Alpha, the man I would follow anywhere, anytime.

"I am! But where to?"

"Home."

I turned the truck onto the highway and headed back in the direction of our pack.

Our *all-male* pack.

What were they going to do when we arrived home with a young, fertile female? There would likely be pandemonium.

"Why'd you grab her, Dex?" I had to ask. "I mean, I know she's hot and everything, but…"

"She's my mate," Dexter said, and I stared at him in the rear vision mirror.

That was how I'd felt when I saw her, but I hadn't believed my initial instincts. I'd put it down to hormones and my general level of horniness. It had been far too long for all of us, me in particular.

"How do you know?"

There had to be a way, other than animal lust.

"I knew it when I saw her. That smile, and her scent. But then I touched her, and the sheer force of the mating call knocked her out. Damn near knocked me off my feet, too."

I couldn't stop the laugh that bubbled up. "Are you serious? She passed out when you touched her?"

Was that really the way to know your mate? I couldn't imagine such a force.

"Yeah… I don't know why, though. The elders never said anything like that would happen. Nothing in the old tales about it. Maybe because she's human?"

While he spoke, Dexter was holding the doctor as he would a baby, stroking her face and looking at her like she was the most precious thing in the world.

Envy clawed through my heart like a wolf after its prey. I'd been to every major city within two hours' drive of our town. Slept with dozens of women, all in the fruitless search for a mate.

Then Dexter managed to waltz in and find her at the hospital where his father was being treated. What were the odds?

"Well, what are we going to do with her when we get back to the pack?"

"I have no idea, but I couldn't just leave her there, on the floor of the waiting area," Dexter said.

I agreed with him. If I'd found my mate, the last thing I'd do is drive away from her.

Jay piped up from the seat next to me. "But, she's human. How is it possible to have a human mate? I mean, we've talked about the possibility, but did any of you actually expect to find your fated mate in a human?"

The question hung in the air like a prayer, until Dex and I both shook our heads. "I hoped, kinda," I admitted. "But I never really thought..."

Jay cleared his throat again, his nervousness making my own skin tingle. "Ah... do you think it's possible that she could be all of our mates, Dex?"

The Alpha growled in a possessive way. Clearly, he did not like that idea one bit. "What do you mean?"

Jay looked at me and I glanced over to him for a moment. The kid had balls saying such a thing to Dexter, but I knew where he was coming from. There was something special about this woman, possibly for all three of us.

And it definitely wasn't my imagination.

I moved my focus back to the road, taking my cue from the Omega and gathering the courage to speak my mind.

"I think Jay means that we all felt a connection when she walked toward us. That call, the chemistry. Do you think it's possible that our pack may have just one mate?"

It was a hard thing for me to say, much less wrap my head around.

When Dexter didn't answer, instead looking confused, I continued. "Not that it's what we really want, Dex. We've always expected to each have our own mates, if we're lucky enough to find them, but the pack has changed. Maybe the legends have, too? I don't know why exactly... but I do know that I wanted her the moment I saw her as well. The only reason I left to get the truck was because you commanded it. And I almost ignored you, even though you are the Alpha."

Dexter looked from his mate to me, to Jay, then back again to the doctor laying in his lap.

For a moment he clutched her fiercely, bringing her close to his chest, anger pulsing over his face, but then he sighed, seeming to relax a little.

"I... can't answer that, Taylor," he admitted gruffly. "I suppose we'll find out when she wakes up."

I looked at my Alpha in the mirror again, guilt gnawing at my chest over the conflict I'd caused for our pack.

"Well, when she wakes, I want to shake her hand, too," I said, trying to alleviate some of the tension in the vehicle with a half-joke. "If she passes out again then we'll know that she's meant for all of us, I suppose."

No one laughed.

Dexter nodded slowly, though he didn't say anything.

Alphas didn't share their women.

Never. No one shared their mate.

Or, they certainly hadn't done so in the past.

I was experiencing anger and conflict myself. It burned in my skin, my heart, and right at my very core.

These two men were my pack mates, and jealousy was eating me up already.

I could only imagine how Dexter must be feeling. Whatever I had burning in my gut, as Alpha, he probably had it magnified ten-fold.

And all of this was contingent on her permitting us to share her. Or even agreeing to stay with us in the first place. Being human meant she would likely fight our ways, and our wolves.

I chuckled, stating the inevitable. "You know what she's going to do when she realizes we're wolf shifters? Run for the hills. No human will accept everything about us. We're paranormal creatures, and monsters to many humans. So why would Fate do this to us?"

Dexter shook his head. "Don't ask me."

We spent the rest of the trip in silence, though Jay tried to chatter and keep us occupied, as he always did. But the unease within all of us was obvious. Even my wolf was on edge.

What would this mean for our family?

Would she turn us away?

Reject us?

Would Dexter fight us for the right to have her to himself?

The unknown future was vast and quite possibly full of terrible things to come.

Once we reached our pack land borders without anyone catching us up, I began to breathe a little easier. I drove through the pack gates and along the long, winding driveway that led to the heart of our village.

What were the elders going to say when they found out what we'd done?

I parked the truck behind our home and turned off the engine. "I'll go unlock the house. You carry her inside. It'll be better if no one else sees her for now."

Dexter nodded and I snuck out of the truck, opening the back door and praying no one had caught sight of us yet.

I had the strangest need to protect and hide the woman Dexter had stolen. If she wasn't my mate as well as Dex's, I'd be shocked.

I opened the door and held it wide with my body.

Dexter got out of the truck and hurried into the house with the beauty in his arms and Jay close on his heels.

"Put her in Jay's room," I suggested, just as Dexter went to ascend the stairs, obviously about to take her to his bedroom.

We had a four-bedroom, double-story house that we'd built together when we'd first joined into our own pack ten years ago. Each of us had a bedroom, and the fourth was set up as a home office with the possibility of converting into a future nursery.

A dream we had feared would never come true.

"Why?" Dexter called out, his tone a touch aggressive.

"Because it's the least threatening," I answered as I brushed past him to open the door.

My point must have been valid because, after a moment, Dexter walked past me and placed her gently on Jay's queen-sized bed.

The colors in the room were blue and white, non-threatening and relaxing.

My room had a red and black theme, while Dexter had silver bedding and heavy wooden furniture. I could only imagine what Claire would think if she woke up in one of the latter two rooms.

Dexter backed away from the sleeping beauty and we all headed into the kitchen to talk about the next step in our non-existent plan.

I wasn't sure why she was still asleep. It wasn't normal to pass out for so long, surely? But what did I know about human anatomy and exposure to the fated mate pull?

Jay grabbed three beers from the fridge, popped the lids and handed them out.

I chugged half of mine down in a few gulps, my thirst stronger than I realized.

When I put down the drink, I glanced toward Jay's bedroom once again.

"Did we just kidnap someone?"

Dexter began to pace and growl in a strange way. "I need to shift and run. I can't hold it together much longer. But someone needs to stay here with her."

Jay began to strip, shedding his clothes in record time. "I'll go with you. I've been itching to shift since I first saw her at the hospital."

Dexter stared at him. "Me, too... so that probably means that... maybe it is possible to actually share a mate..."

They looked at me and I raised my hands. "I wouldn't mind a run, but I'm more antsy to stay here with her. I'm happy to stand guard until you get back."

And it was true. Though my shifter circled within my mind, he was more settled than Jay or Dexter seemed to be. Which was interesting. Perhaps I hadn't bonded to her in the way I'd thought?

Only seeing her conscious and awake would answer that question.

Dexter pulled his tank over his head and pushed his black jeans to the ground.

"Thanks. We won't be long."

I watched as my human pack morphed into wolves and bounded out of the house and toward the woodlands that surrounded our home.

Dexter was silver, Jay was brown. I was black when in wolf form, and we all made the perfect triad of colors. One of the many reasons we knew we were a perfect, balanced pack. The fur never lied.

I crept over to Jay's bedroom door, unable to stay away. I watched our mate sleep for a moment, then shook my head at how she'd feel if she woke up and found a strange man standing over her. As I walked away the thought occurred to me.

What had I just said? *Our mate...*

I was getting ahead of myself here, and was still confused about how it had all happened anyway. I hadn't known it was possible to have one woman complete a triad of wolves.

Maybe it wasn't possible. But honestly, it made perfect sense to me when I thought about it. Why wouldn't a pack be designed to protect one precious woman?

Though the sharing element of it all... a growl rolled through my chest that I couldn't control.

I wasn't too sure how that was going to work out.

Dexter would be the worst, the most jealous of us, of course. He was dominant and aggressive by nature—possessive, in fact. I wasn't much better.

Jay would go along with whatever we all wanted, as he always did. But it was nice to see him looking enthusiastic and uncharacteristically *wolf like* today. As an Omega, he tended to be the smallest and softest us of all, but not today.

Obviously, our mate brought out the best in us.

My keen hearing picked up a feminine gasp and shuffling movement from Jay's room. With my heart thumping in my chest as anticipation wound around me, I grabbed a bottle of water from the fridge and called out to her.

"Come out and have some water, Doc."

My heart pounded harder as I heard her moving about. I didn't even know her name, which was terrible. I should have asked Dexter more questions about her before he left.

She popped her head around the doorway, her eyes wide and the smell of fear catching sharp in my nose.

I stayed on my side of the kitchen bench, not wanting to frighten her by moving any closer.

But my wolf was rising, I could feel it in the heat of my skin and the way my arms trembled with both weakness and strength.

My Beta wolf recognised its mate, and human or not, my shifter didn't care.

She's mine.

I grabbed hold of the bench in front of me and forced a calm smile to my face. I was happy to see her, more than happy. That was the problem.

But I didn't want to scare her any more than I probably was going to anyway.

As she crept out of Jay's bedroom, all I could think about was stripping her clear of her hospital scrubs and taking her on the floor boards beneath my feet.

I'd been dreaming about my mate for as long as I could remember. And to finally be within reach of knowing the feeling of her wrapped around me, to feel her love and her heart beating against mine... it would be heaven.

"Where am I?" she asked, her hands clenching into fists at her sides as though she couldn't decide if she needed to fight her way out of here or not.

She was pale, and obviously still in shock.

I wasn't sure how to approach her. We wanted her to stay, not run from us. But how to do that?

"You're in the Woodlands. I'm Taylor."

She didn't seem to hear me, or respond, so I poured some cold water into a glass and pushed it across the bench.

"Here, have a drink. You fainted."

"I fainted?" she asked, coming forward and frowning as though she didn't believe me.

"Yes. At the hospital."

She put a hand to her forehead. "Oh, yes. I kind of remember that. I was talking to a man about his father and..."

"And you fainted."

"So why am I here?"

She looked at me expectantly and suddenly our reasons for bringing her back here didn't seem so straightforward.

And they certainly wouldn't make any sense to a human.

What was the best lie I could come up with, that was kind of close to the truth?

"Ah... you were talking to Dex at the time, about his dad, and when you dropped into his arms he kind of panicked and decided to bring you home to make sure you were okay."

Her eyes narrowed with what looked like anger this time, the bright blue irises flickering with fire.

Something inside of me cackled with delight. She was a feisty one. Good. She was going to need that heat if she was going to live out here with us.

"Why would he do that? I was at the hospital. They would have taken care of me."

I needed to cut off this conversation until Dexter returned. I was liable to stuff everything up and then where would we be? With a mate who didn't want us.

"Dex will explain everything when he gets back. He won't be long. But for the moment, I should introduce myself. I'm Taylor." I repeated my name, and this time I saw the words register. She was obviously coming more fully to her senses.

I held out my hand in a non-threatening manner and began to move around the island bench so that I could touch her for the first time. Would she faint on me as she had with Dexter? Or would she continue to stare at me with the fear I saw in her eyes when she first peered around the door frame?

"Taylor, this all sounds very dodgy," she said. "Are you sure I'm not dreaming? Because this isn't making any sense."

I kept my hand out and waited. "I still don't know your name, Doctor."

Her shoulders dropped a little as though she was letting down her guard for the first time. "It's Claire."

Claire. What a beautiful name. She reached out and shook my hand, and electrical currents of sensation coursed through my arm.

Claire's eyes went wide and then her eyes shut. She began to fall to the floor and I dove forward with both arms out.

I caught her just before her head hit the coffee table and swung her up into my arms, loving the feeling of her weight against my body.

The front door slammed shut behind me and I turned toward Dexter and Jay, who were still naked and panting hard from their run.

"Well, that answers *that* question," Dexter said, his tone begrudging.

I looked up at him. "What do you mean?"

"That's what happened when I touched her, too. She's obviously your mate as well."

I smiled at my Alpha. "Our pack's mate, Dex. Told you."

Dexter nodded once and I carried Claire back into Jay's bedroom and laid her on the bed once again. I adjusted her limbs a little, to ensure she wouldn't be uncomfortable when she woke. Again.

When I walked back into the lounge, Jay and Dexter had their jeans on and I felt ten feet tall. I'd found my mate, and she was as beautiful as I'd always imagined she'd be.

"What are you smirking about?" Dexter asked as he cracked open a beer.

He was tense and I knew jealousy, like any other monster, was going to shred him if we didn't cut it off at the knees.

"I'm in shock. After all these years... I can't believe we finally found our mate. We're the first pack in the entire Woodlands area to find her, Dex. You have to see how amazing that is."

The Alpha's lips tweaked up at the edges. "Yeah, I can kinda see that."

"And if you think about all the reasons we're arranged into triad packs, it makes sense that the three of us are meant to make one woman perfectly happy."

Dexter took a swig of his beer and looked at me. "What do you mean?"

Jay sidled up next to me. "You're probably right, Taylor. I mean... I always wondered why the elders would do such a thing. To deliberately create every mini-pack to have an Alpha, Beta and Omega. What was the real reason other than to stop all the Alphas fighting amongst themselves? This means that our mate..."

He trailed off and I realized that, like me before she woke up, Jay didn't know her name.

"Claire."

Jay grinned. "Claire..." He said her name slowly, like he was savoring the taste of her. "She will have a perfect family unit. An Alpha to protect her, a Beta to build a home for her, and me, an Omega, to be her best friend and probably the one who looks after all the kids when they come, since she's a doctor. She'll probably want to keep working... and stuff."

Jay stopped talking as we stared at him in awe. Jay could be quiet, so I didn't always give him the appreciation he deserved. He was smart and had enough heart for the whole family.

"What? You know I've always wanted loads of kids around."

I moved my gaze over to Dexter's and our eyes met with an understanding. Sure, we'd always wanted kids, but we didn't want to hang around the house all day with them.

We wanted to work, provide for our family and the community. If our mate was an extremely intelligent, working woman, who would look after our house and the kids?

Jay.

Dexter cleared his throat. "Maybe you're right."

I nodded, trying not to let my happiness shine through my massive smile *too* much.

"So how are we going to convince her to stay, then? She's human, for one thing, and I can tell you, when she woke up, she wasn't too impressed that we brought her back here instead of leaving her at the hospital."

Dexter grinned. "It's simple. We seduce her into staying."

Jay stared at Dexter wide-eyed, but I was more sceptical.

"Seriously?"

Dexter nodded. "What woman wouldn't want the love and attention of three men?"

"At once?" I asked, trying to clarify the rules and intent.

I'd tried not to think about how we were going to share her sexually.

He shrugged. "Yeah, why not? If she's destined to be the mate to a full pack, then she'll have an appetite to match."

I grinned at my Alpha, lust heating up my blood.

"I like the sound of that."

4

CLAIRE

Oh. My. God.

Did those guys just say they were going to share me between all three of them? As in... sexually?

Like some footy slut on a team trip? All three of them at once?

No fucking way!

I managed to sit up and swing my legs over the side of the bed without alerting them. They were too busy discussing how they were going to keep me, to listen for my movement anyway.

Keep me!

Like I was a bloody stray puppy they found by the side of the road.

And what was with all the Alpha, pack... crap? They talked like they were a bunch of primitive animals—which they must be, if they were thinking of enslaving me.

Me! The girl no one *ever* wants!

I got to my feet and looked around the room for a weapon. Anything I could use to defend myself if necessary.

These guys sounded absolutely insane.

Who kidnaps a fainting woman straight out of a hospital and then takes her home to keep?

Psychopaths! That's who.

The room I'd been sleeping in was too bland for my taste, and other than a few books, there was nothing to throw. Not even a baseball bat to swing.

The window!

I tiptoed to the sash window and quietly opened the curtains. I could try to climb out and run away, but where the hell was I? All I could see outside was grass, and then woodlands surrounding the house.

I wasn't in the city any longer, that was for sure.

And if I did try and run anyway, would I be just jumping from the frying pan into the fire?

Because, although those men were talking about seducing me into staying with them, I had the strangest feeling that they wouldn't hurt me. Which was crazy. They had kidnapped me. They weren't normal men, so who knew what they'd do, if I tried to escape.

What did I know? I'd done only a brief stint in mental health during my residency and knew as much now as I did before the rotation.

"Oh, you're awake. Great."

I yelped and spun around as someone spoke to me from the doorway.

It was the one I hadn't met yet. I'd heard his voice out there, and wondered what he was like. He'd sounded... gentler than the others, somehow. He was much smaller than the other two, and had a radiant smile I hadn't expected.

"Who are you?" I asked, scanning this one for any signs of danger.

He was very pretty rather than handsome, and not much taller than me. But there was something very sexy about him as well. His smile said that he'd go to the ends of the earth to bring me my heart's desire.

I shook myself to dispel the romantic nonsense. I should be terrified right now but instead, I was entranced by the sight of this guy's amazing abs.

Why didn't he have a shirt on?

"I'm Jay. This is my bedroom. Do you need anything? Food? A beer? You must be feeling pretty strange at the moment."

His voice was calm, but strong. My whole body instantly relaxed. Maybe this one would give me a straight answer.

"Why am I here, Jay? And what keeps happening to me? At the hospital I fainted, and I think I fainted again just now."

Jay smiled and took a step back. "Come on out. I promise, no one here will ever hurt you. We can talk through what happened, and why."

I took a few steps toward the bedroom door, though my logical mind screamed at me to run.

Run hard, run fast, and don't look back.

But something deeper, more innate and instinctual wanted to trust this beautiful man before me.

So, despite my misgivings and the screaming of the modern woman in my head, I crept forward, until I was standing in the doorway once again.

There were two other men in the room, and I recognized both of them.

Dexter, the big brute from the hospital whose father was unwell. He was half-naked as well, and my gaze did an instant inspection of his massive chest and abs.

I almost groaned aloud.

Why does he have to be so damn attractive?

I looked away from the guys in front of me, heat coursing up my face, mostly due to embarrassment. I'd been perving on them in a most unprofessional way. Perving on the guys who had snatched me from the hospital. What was wrong with me?

Dexter was larger than a professional footballer, and so much more cut. There wasn't a scrap of fat on him.

"Don't you gentlemen own shirts?"

"Oh, sorry," Dexter said. "We forgot you humans care about that stuff."

My head came up at that one. "Humans? What do you mean?" I narrowed my eyes at him. "What are you guys, if not human?"

Okay, so I needed to revise my thoughts. These guys really were nutters.

I glanced from one to the other, then back to Jay. Dexter picked up a tank from the floor and pulled it on, then threw Jay one too.

Jay pulled on the top and came forward, holding out his hand with a grin. "Nice to meet you officially, Claire."

I looked at his hand suspiciously. If my foggy memory was correct, shaking the last two guys' hands was what instigated the fainting.

Which made no logical sense. So, what was I afraid of?

"Okay." I reached out and put my palm to his.

Pulses of pleasure coursed up my arm and my knees went weak.

Oh, no. Not again.

Jay surged forward and caught me before I hit the ground. But I didn't pass out this time. Instead, I was caught in his eyes.

Blue pools of magic and wonder.

I wanted to kiss him. I could feel it in my very bones.

My gaze dropped to his lips. His mouth was beautiful and so close to me.

And as he dropped his head and stole my breath, I floated up to the ceiling and watched myself kiss him back.

My rational brain couldn't believe I was doing it—letting a complete stranger kiss me like that. But then he slipped his tongue into my mouth and I was back in my body, feeling everything.

The heat of his thin, muscled body beneath my hands. His lips pressing passionately against mine. The taste of his tongue inside my mouth making me moan like a wanton slut.

It had been far too long since anyone had kissed me at all, let alone like *that.*

But then his strong hands moved to my ass, gripping my flesh and pulling me closer against his cock, which was hard beneath his jeans.

His flesh pressed against my belly, pulling me back to reality and the great big warning bell clanging in my head.

This was dangerous... and wrong. So wrong.

I broke away from his grip, breathing hard. I stood up and stepped back, holding my hand up so he didn't approach again.

I could feel the energy in the room, the heat. The atmosphere had changed, becoming charged.

I could actually smell their arousal. Their need for me. All three of them. And worse, I could feel my own arousal, slick between my legs.

They all made as if to step toward me and I pushed my hand out more firmly. "No. Please. Don't touch me!"

The three of them froze and Jay held up both hands. "No one will touch you, Claire. Not if you don't want it. You don't need to fear us."

Dexter growled, the sound both scary and strangely exciting. I could feel the wetness between my thighs, readying my body for their entrance.

No! I wasn't doing this.

I focused on Jay, reaching for my anger simmering just beneath the surface. "Oh, really? You kidnapped me! There's three of you and only one of me. You could rape me and kill me and no one would be the wiser! How can I not be afraid of you right now?"

Angry tears filled my eyes as I suddenly realized how vulnerable I was. Dexter took a step forward and I yelped.

"Not you! You're the scariest one of all."

Dexter fell back, his face a mask of hurt and distress.

Jay moved in front of Dexter to block him from my view, and my heart that had been racing like a steam train began to calm down.

"Claire, seriously. We would never hurt you. We couldn't. That would be like cutting off our own arm."

He seemed sincere, and I was a pretty adept at identifying a liar.

"Okay, well if that's true, you'll take me home. Now."

I put my hands on my hips to emphasise how serious I was and Jay's smile faded.

"Um... but we haven't even gotten to know you yet."

Pardon me?

"What do you mean? Why would you want to get to know me?"

Didn't he hear how insane he sounded?

"Um..." Jay didn't seem to have an answer for that.

Taylor stepped up next to Jay and got my attention, but didn't approach me, which was good.

"There's something special about you... for us. In our community we believe in love at first sight. Fated mates."

"Mates?" They made me sound like an animal. "Who are you guys? What are you?" I'm not sure why I added that last sentence, but it seemed appropriate, somehow.

Taylor looked at the other men, who both appeared reluctant to answer me honestly. I huffed out in frustration.

"You've gotta tell me, because you're starting to freak me out."

Taylor frowned. "You won't be able to handle the truth."

I glared at him. "Listen, mate, I'm a physician. I can handle anything you guys throw at me. Because all I want is the truth. That's very important to me."

After dealing for years with boyfriends who'd lied and cheated their way through our relationships, the last thing I wanted was more dishonest men.

Dexter moved to take a step forward and Taylor grabbed his arm.

Dexter frowned, that pained look on his face returning once again.

He looked at me and took a step back. "You don't need to fear me, Claire. All this..." He indicated to his body. "Is to protect you. That's what I'm built for—protection. I'd never hurt you. I'd do anything to keep you safe."

I held his gaze for a moment and eventually nodded. I could kind of understand that. But any men whom I'd met in the past who were as big as Dexter were real meat-heads. They cared only for looks and intimidation.

"Okay... well, then tell me what this is all about. And don't hold anything back."

The men shared a look again and finally Taylor stepped forward.

"Okay, but you may want to sit down."

Really?

I gave them a look that clearly said, "Are you serious right now?" but when they didn't move, I eventually threw up my hands and sat on the couch.

"Fine. But you guys need to sit down, too. It's like being surrounded by massive trees."

They all found a seat so fast I barely saw them move. Taylor on the couch, Jay on the edge of a chair and Dexter, who seemed to have taken my fear of him to heart, and moved all the way back to the stairs that I assumed led up to a second floor.

It was really strange, but seeing Dexter so sad and far away from the rest of us hurt me in the weirdest way. It was like a hand was being pressed to my sternum and applying extreme pressure.

I wanted him closer. But why would I, when he was by far the most intimidating of all the men? None of this made any sense.

I sat up straighter and steeled myself for a revelation.

"Okay, hit me with it. What is this about? And what have I got to do with it all?"

Taylor shifted forward on his seat and once again, I was struck with how beautiful these men were, each of them in their own way, but all incredibly sexy.

Taylor was hot, in the way men who graced the front of magazines were hot. His hair was shaggy, long and touchable. His eyelashes were far too long for a man, only on him they looked fantastic, and his shoulders were so wide, they left no doubt as to how strong he was.

Taylor grinned. "You feel that attraction between us?"

What could I do?

Lie?

When I'd just lectured them on how important honesty was to me, and when I was so obviously perving on them.

"Yeah... so what?"

That didn't actually *mean* anything.

He smirked at me. "Are you attracted to all three of us?"

I didn't even need to look at the other two men. "Yes," I admitted shortly. "But what's that got to do with anything?"

That couldn't be unusual. After all, they were seriously attractive men.

Taylor laughed. "Is that a normal reaction for you? To want to have sex with the only three men in the room?"

I gasped involuntarily. I didn't want to....

I sat back against the couch, crossed my legs and arms over my body and stared him down.

When he put it like that... "Well, no. But..." But what? I let my arms drop down, folding my hands in my lap. "Yeah, it is weird, actually. I haven't been attracted to anyone in... forever."

I shrugged, not wanting to get into the reasons for my lack of sex life.

Dexter got to his feet and began to pace at the back of the room. I could feel his aggression, his pent-up emotions. But they didn't seem to be directed at me.

"Keep going, Taylor," he said, not looking at me as he stalked up and down like a lion at the zoo.

I looked over at Taylor. "Tell me."

Taylor pressed his lips together and then spoke. "Okay. Well, the three of us are wolf shifters."

He couldn't be telling me they were some mythical being that belonged in the movies. "You mean... like werewolves or something?"

It was in *Twilight*, so why not? Right?

He smiled. "Not quite. We aren't a slave to the moon and we

have complete control over our bodies, even in wolf form. Jay, Dex and I are a triad pack. We're part of a much larger pack as well. The Woodlands Pack."

These guys obviously needed their heads examined.

"So, let me get this right. You believe you're a wolf shifter... hmm... okay, then. Show me."

I knew, from a mental health perspective, I wasn't meant to shatter their illusions too quickly, but I was running out of time. Everyone at the hospital would be looking for me, and within a few days, my parents would start to worry, too.

I lived alone, so there wasn't a roommate or a husband to note my absence, which I wasn't going to admit to these guys. But I had to work out how I was going to get home from here and the easiest way was to get them to drive me back to the hospital and drop me there.

Taylor looked over at the other men in the room. "Um... I suppose Jay could show you. He's the smallest of us. Dex's wolf is pretty big."

Jay looked at me with big, wide eyes. "Are you sure you want me to do that, Claire?"

I wanted to laugh, but managed not to. These guys couldn't be serious right now. "Yeah. Go for it." I waved my hands in the air, giving him permission to do whatever he was about to do.

Although, if a real wolf materialized into this room, I might just end up shitting myself.

He began to undress and moved behind the couch. "Okay... but don't yell, okay?"

I nodded and Jay disappeared as though he'd never been there.

"Holy shit." I jumped to my feet. "Where'd he go?"

Around the couch stepped a small brown wolf.

"Oh my God!"

I jumped up onto the couch, shrieking a little as adrenaline thundered through my veins.

"Hey, stop. You said you wouldn't yell," Taylor said, as the brown wolf disappeared behind the couch once again.

"He's timid in his wolf form; you've gotta be quieter than that,"

Dexter said as well, his tone one that was protective of Jay and clearly a little annoyed at me.

For the first time I saw the link between the men. The family element. The brotherhood.

"Um... that's Jay?" I asked, pointing to the couch.

"We told you," Taylor said.

I swallowed hard. This was really happening. "Okay... what should I do, then?"

Should I apologize? Ask him to come back again?

"Well, maybe sit down and call him to you. If you want to be comfortable with us in both forms, I suppose you'll have to get used to it."

I was pretty sure I had no intention of being comfortable with them in any form. But what choice did I have at this point in time? "Um... okay. Jay, can you come around, please?"

The head of the wolf popped around the couch again and my stomach tightened.

Oh my God. It was a real wolf. I couldn't explain anything about this whole experience, but there was no doubting the animal that stared at me unblinkingly.

"Um... okay. Can I... pet him?" I asked Taylor, though the amount of sharp, pointed teeth in the wolf's mouth had me questioning my own sanity.

Taylor nodded. "Yeah. Absolutely. Go for it."

Taylor ran his hand over the back of the brown wolf, who was slowly walking toward me.

He had the biggest, most soulful eyes I'd ever seen on an animal and once again, I felt my anxiety drain away.

He stepped closer and I extended my hand to him, though my arm trembled and my chest burned from my inability to breathe.

He put his wet nose against my fingers and then licked my hand. I squealed with surprise this time and pulled my hand back.

Taylor laughed and the wolf backed away behind the couch.

I blinked and suddenly Jay was standing there again. Naked, and pulling on his clothes.

I stared, unable to speak.

What sort of world had I stumbled across here?

5

JAY

I pulled my top over my head and quickly buttoned my jeans. Adrenaline was pumping through my muscles so fast they trembled with strength and unease. I had the strongest urge to go outside, shift back into my wolf form and go running again.

But I didn't want to leave my mate, because that was certainly who she was. Sure, she may not have fainted at the touch of my skin on hers, but she'd kissed me. That was even better.

And as I glanced back toward my Alpha, I could see he knew Claire was mine as much as his and Taylor's. He was pissed that I'd gotten in first, but I shrugged. Could he really blame me for taking advantage when it was offered?

I walked back around the couch, presentable once more for the human.

"I... um..." Claire didn't seem to be able to speak, but at least she wasn't running from the house screaming, or passing out again.

"Are you okay?" I asked her as I settled down onto the couch arm.

I struggled not to stare at her. She was so beautiful. So clean and lush and just... amazing.

Her hair was the color of sunshine, with tips of gold. It had been

40

all pulled back into a harsh style at the hospital, but was now tumbling down around her face.

"Ah... um. So, you can all do that?" she asked, her face pale.

I nodded. "Yes, everyone in the pack can."

Claire swallowed hard, her throat and face pulling and working with her stress.

"Um... everyone? Even the kids? The women?"

I glanced at Taylor. How were we going to answer that? Honesty was probably the best answer. She had said she wanted honesty, above all else.

"Um..."

Taylor stepped up. "Our mothers and aunts... yes, they can shift, though they don't much, anymore. They're getting a bit past it."

Claire glanced from me to Taylor. "What about your sisters? Girlfriends?"

I cleared my throat. We had to tell her the truth. "Our pack hasn't had a female shifter born in over fifty years."

Claire stared at me like I'd grown two heads. "Are you serious?"

"Yes."

She fell back against the couch and exhaled. "Whoa. That's crazy."

I nodded because I totally agreed with her. "So, we have a whole town full of three-man packs, and no women. No children."

Her eyes that had been glazed over and unfocused, snapped into place. "Hang on a second. Do you think that I... please tell me you didn't grab me so that I could fill the gap for you? I do not want some wolfie... woodsman. I don't want any man!"

I heard Taylor's chuckle and Dexter's growl and jumped to my feet.

"We understand, Claire. But in our community, we all have a true mate. Soul mates, in a way. Fate destined."

"Yeah, so?" Claire said, flicking her hair back out of her eyes. But she was nervous. More nervous than she had been, all of a sudden. Was it my mention of soul mates? Did she feel the connection, too?

And if so, was she going to try and deny it, when the evidence was right there in front of us all?

I swallowed hard. Was I the one who should tell her?

Dexter got to his feet and walked over to the back of the couch, staring down at our beautiful woman. "So, you're *our* mate, Claire. Not mine, or Taylor's, or Jay's. All of ours. You're designed for us, and we're destined for you."

Claire jumped to her feet and pushed both her hands out in front of her like she could stop our words and everything she was hearing.

"Stop right there."

She took several breaths, her cheeks flushing with blood, making her look even more desirable.

And aroused.

"I am *not* a mate, to anyone. Let alone three men who can turn into wolves."

She was shaking her head, like she had no idea how this had all happened. And then she couldn't seem to stop shaking her head.

Taylor stepped forward, his heart on his sleeve. "Claire, you have no idea how lucky we are to have found you."

"No. *No!*" She was yelling now and a tiny part of me wished Dexter would make her pass out again.

Her hysteria was making my stomach tie itself up in knots.

"Stop, please. No one is going to hurt you," I tried, in a placating tone.

She fixed me with an angry stare. "Then you'll take me home. *Now*. Because if you don't... If you don't..."

Dexter chuckled and leaned against the couch, his arms crossed. "You'll what?"

Claire's face darkened and it made me proud to see that she wasn't scared of us. Quite the opposite actually.

I glanced over to where Dexter leaned with a deceptive casualness. He might look calm, but he was vibrating with energy, just like Taylor and me. We were all feeding off the tension emanating from Claire and her temper.

Dexter's arms were huge, his biceps the size of Claire's thighs. Did she seriously think she had any hope of fighting any of us off, if we were so inclined to hold her here against her will?

"I'll never forgive you for keeping me here. If I am some special soul mate person to you, do you really want me pissed off at you for the rest of my life? And that's if you can watch me twenty-four-seven. As soon as you're asleep, I'll run away. I can promise you that." She was practically hissing now.

I couldn't handle much more of this. The air was practically sparking, from all the overblown emotion in the room. From all of us.

I twisted around and stared at my Alpha and Beta, whose hackles were rising at the threat.

"Taylor, why don't you go see your parents? And Dex, catch up with your mom. Tell her about your dad's operation, and then maybe explain about Claire, and come back in an hour? I need to speak to her. Alone."

I didn't assert myself too often in our pack. I didn't need to. Dexter and Taylor did a great job of looking after us. But as I saw them register my words, I was glad I had chosen this battle to speak up. Because now they were listening to me.

"Ah..." Dexter began, then paused. "I do need to let Mom know, about Dad, and that he's going to be all right once the stents go in." His gaze was sheepish. In the shock of finding our fated mate, other priorities had dimmed.

I tilted my head toward the door.

Dex backed away without argument, and my respect for my Alpha grew. He was placing his trust in me, and I would make sure that trust was not misplaced.

Taylor followed, with only a long, hard look at me, and as they shut the door behind them and walked from the house, I turned back to our mate. Her shoulders were up almost to her ears and she looked far too stressed.

"Can we talk, Claire? I promise I won't hurt you."

She stared at me, as if debating something within herself.

"Do you want something to eat?" I prompted. "We don't have a lot of your city processed food, but we keep a good supply of meat and fruit and fresh things here."

I moved toward the kitchen, pulling out some berries from the fridge—berries that had been fresh picked from our fields.

"Ah... um..." She stumbled into the kitchen and pulled up a stool. "I suppose."

She noticed the variety of berries we had, their color and size not what normal supermarkets would carry.

"You grow everything here yourselves?"

I nodded and pushed the bowl toward her. "We're pretty self-sustainable. We have to go into nearby towns like Little Creek for some things, of course, but we try to stay off the grid as much as possible."

We had solar power for heating and electricity, farmed fields of crops, and we raised chickens and cows for meat, milk and eggs.

Our ancestors had done a good job of keeping our community safe and sustainable, and it was on my generation to keep that sustainability going.

Claire picked up a berry and bit into it. A soft moan surfacing from her lips made me groan in unison.

Her gaze caught mine and I shrugged. "Sorry. Your reactions are linked to mine. I can't control it. You get enjoyment from eating a berry, then I feel it, too."

She sighed, letting her shoulders fall. And when she looked at me, the sadness on her face broke my heart.

"Claire, please don't look at me like that. You're not defeated, you're not trapped. This is a blessing. I wish you could see it that way. We all need to work out the best way through the situation."

I hadn't realized how hard it would be for a human to understand us. I'd never had to think about it before today.

She looked at me with pleading eyes. "Please, Jay. You seem to be the most sensible of them all. Take me home. Please. Drop me off at the hospital and I swear I won't tell anyone what happened. Not about Dexter kidnapping me, or you guys turning into wolves. None of it."

I smiled at her, to hide my consternation. She still wanted to leave? Then her eyebrows flew up, a horror-filled expression crossing her face.

"Unless... oh, God. Do you have to kill me now that I know your secret?"

Kill her? I burst out laughing. I couldn't help it; the idea was too ludicrous to entertain.

"Claire, seriously. This isn't the movies. We're not the mob. And even if you wanted to tell the world, who would believe you? That's not our concern."

Well, in a way it was. It was forbidden to tell the outside world about us, but did that apply to humans who found out about us? The whole area was gray, given this was my first experience of sharing anything about our life as shifters, with a human.

That was the last thing I was worried about at this point in time.

"What is your concern, then?" she asked quietly.

I sighed.

"Look, Claire, whether you believe us or not, you're the woman we're meant to be with. Me, Dexter, and Taylor. There is no one else for us, and there can't be anyone else for us. Not now that we've met you. Don't you understand? If you don't want us, then you can leave and we'll live here, just the three of us, forever. On our own."

And although yesterday I was relatively settled with the idea of the three of us being a family unit forever, today was different.

Today I didn't want to settle for less.

Today I knew the truth.

Humans were going to save our pack from extinction. New blood was necessary to keep us strong and help us survive.

Whether or not the elders had known that, when they broke us off into mini-packs of three men, was moot. *Something* had been guiding our pack in the right direction, and finding Claire had been a lightbulb moment in that regard.

Perhaps that had been the plan all along?

She gave me a strange smile. "That sounds... totally bonkers. You know that, Jay?"

I shrugged. "Maybe to you, but that's how we were brought up. One true mate for all of us. I mean, we did think we'd have one true mate each, but once we met you and felt the bond, we knew it wasn't going to be like that. You are our true mate, and we will need to learn how to live with that. So, yes... this is something different, even for us. For one, you're not a wolf shifter, and two, there's only one of you and three of us. Neither is the norm as far as our experience goes, but I'm sure you can handle us."

I gave her the sexiest grin I had in my arsenal and redness flooded her cheeks. She looked down as if embarrassed.

But she didn't say anything to negate what I'd said.

"You can feel it too, can't you?" I asked her. "You can feel the connection, the need, the desire?"

She still wouldn't look at me and I reached over and lifted her chin with one of my fingers.

Electricity sizzled through our connection, but in a muted, comfortable way.

When her gaze lifted to connect with mine, I smiled at her. "Don't be afraid of us. We will *never* hurt you."

She sighed heavily and jerked her chin out of my grasp. "It's not that I'm afraid, exactly. It's just that this is... well... crazy! I'm a logical woman. Cold and calculating if any of my ex-boyfriends are to be believed."

A growl rattled through me at the idea of her bedding other men. Men who failed to see the beautiful, sexy being they had in their grasp.

When she looked at me, I coughed to cover it up, but the possessive wolf in me raised his head.

6

———

JAY

"Sorry... Anyway. You aren't crazy. I can guarantee you that. And if you're designed for us—all three of us—you really must be the most remarkable woman."

She stopped shaking her head and looked at me properly.

"What do you mean?"

I stared at Claire for a moment and realized that this was the key. The words, the compliments. She was beginning to open up like a flower ready to drink in the rain.

How deprived had she been of such words? Affection, too, perhaps? The men she had met before must have been imbeciles.

"Would you sit with me on the couch? I promise I won't do anything weird."

She smiled and wiped at a stray tear that fell down her cheek. "Okay."

I took her hand, loving the feel of the pulses of pleasure such a small touch brought, and took her to the couch.

I pushed my luck and sat first, then pulled her onto my lap.

She landed awkwardly and although she moved away a little, she stayed with her legs draped across my thighs. I was grateful for the

47

contact, and for the fact that she seemed to be building toward a modicum of trust.

"Now look. I don't want to give you a thousand compliments, because you won't believe me yet. But what I will say, is that you are beyond beautiful. Your body is magic and your smile makes me want to drop to my knees and worship you."

She looked down at her hands, but I could see the small smile playing on her lips.

"But there's so much more to you than that, I know. You're a doctor, so I know you are also incredibly intelligent, hardworking and driven. Which will hold you in good stead with our pack, and the women at the Alpha's right hand. They are strong women."

She nodded and joined the conversation again. "I can imagine."

I squeezed her thigh, hiding my smile when I saw her suppress a shiver at my touch. "And if you're designed for three of us, then you'll be twice as strong, twice as courageous. I can see your fire, your temper, and your passion. You are an incredible woman, Claire, and I honestly cannot wait to see what the future brings for us."

She glanced down again and twirled her fingers together. "But I don't know anything about you. Any of you. How can I trust you? How can I possibly stay here and get to know you when I have a job... a life to get back to?"

Relief winged through my heart as she prepared to bargain with me. I could hear it in her tone, see it in the way she looked at me. She was listening to me... she *wanted* to believe me.

Time. We just needed time. To prove to her that we could love her in a way that would make her happy.

"Give us two days. We'll show you our pack, and you can meet the elders. Spend time with us. I promise you won't regret it, and then at the end of the allocated time, if you want to return to the city —we'll take you."

I held my breath against the pain such a statement brought. Take her back?

Never!

Dexter and Taylor would kill me for even offering her the option. But we couldn't force her to stay. That wasn't healthy for anyone. She'd hate us all.

"Ah... I do have the next few days off work. I was planning on catching up on some sleep and seeing my parents."

Yes! Thank you!

"Well, you can definitely sleep and relax here. You can take my bedroom—I'll sleep on the couch. Honestly, we'll do anything to make you happy. You need to see that to believe it, I know."

She looked at me with a sceptical expression. I knew that staying with us was the last thing she wanted to agree to.

"Please, Claire. Stay with us. Don't ignore this opportunity that Fate has presented."

She rolled her eyes at me. "Jay, I don't believe in Fate. No rational human does."

I smiled at her. "You've never seen a patient pull through, when all logic says he or she shouldn't have? Or, perhaps a perfectly healthy patient just passes away in his sleep? You've honestly never seen anything that couldn't be explained away with logic or reason?"

Her lips twisted up and she glanced down at her hands. "Well... yeah, I suppose so. There are always things that happen that can't be totally explained..."

She stopped.

I grinned at her, even though she wasn't looking at me yet. "Trust me when I say that you need to throw everything you thought you knew, out the window. Two days, Claire. Please."

She stared at her hands for a minute longer then finally looked up at me, tears shimmering in her blue eyes and making them shine like sapphires.

I reached up and caressed her cheek, wiping away the moisture on her face.

"Why are you crying? Is your medical mind blown apart by everything you've seen and heard today?"

She nodded and hiccupped. "Yeah, pretty much. I suppose if people can turn into wolves at will, then anything's possible."

"Yes. It is."

I wanted to kiss her again, but did I dare?

She looked up and met my eyes, and suddenly I did dare. I reached over and grabbed her waist, pulling her back onto my lap and pressing my lips to hers.

She gasped against my mouth, but didn't move away.

I didn't rush her, but kept my hands on her waist, though I wanted to explore her body more than anything. I waited and waited, and then I felt it. A softening of her body on mine as she melted toward me.

I gripped her waist tighter and slanted my head so that I could open her lips. She moaned and opened to me. I tasted her tongue with mine once again.

Claire's hands crept up my arms until she was gripping my neck, dragging me into her. I couldn't stand it any longer. I had to get closer.

I pulled at her scrubs, wanting to feel her skin. Needing to remove the barrier between us.

The front door banged loudly and Claire jumped. She moved to slide off my lap but I held her for a moment as I looked toward the entrance.

Dexter and Taylor glowered at me, the rage in their faces clear for the world to see.

Claire began to struggle in earnest and I let her go. She jumped to her feet and I stood up next to her, smiling at my pack.

"Claire has agreed to stay for a few days and get to know us."

The black cloud hanging over Dex and Taylor's heads disappeared instantly.

Taylor stepped forward. "Really? You'll stay?"

I looked over at Claire, whose face was torn with indecision as she bit her lip and didn't speak for a moment. Then she cleared her throat. "You said two days."

I grinned at her and my pack mates. "Yes, I did."

"Claire, how about I show you around the house?" Taylor spoke up.

I didn't want to leave her side, so I added, "Then we can go out for a bit. Meet the pack maybe, if you guys think it'll be safe?"

I looked toward Dexter for guidance.

Our Alpha nodded. "Actually, Mom told me to bring her straight over, for a report on Dad more than anything, I think."

Claire's face changed, her professional persona slipping into place.

"Yes. I'd like to do that, if we can. I don't have any other clothes though, and I suppose you guys have nothing my size?"

The hint of a joke and a tentative smile from Claire made even Dexter grin.

"Ah no... although some of the older women may have some jeans and t-shirts or sweaters near your size," Dex said.

I assessed Claire's figure and guessed maybe a twelve or a fourteen. Perfect for pleasing all three of us.

"Yeah, I'm pretty sure my mom or even one of my aunties will have something for you," I said.

"Great. I'd like to speak to your mom, Dexter."

She walked forward without the fear she'd shown earlier, and I made a mental note that the healer in her was a fierce, protective personality. And that would suit our pack well. If she chose to stay.

"Let's go, then," Dexter said, shooting me another angry look as he ushered her out the door. I had to hide the smile that naturally spread across my face.

I was the only one she'd kissed today so far... but so what?

I was pretty sure that, by the end of the next two days, kisses were not the only things we'd all be sharing.

7

DEXTER

Claire stepped up next to me and the scent of her brought my wolf right up to the surface of my consciousness. I pushed him down with all my might, unwilling to squander the little time we had with her by running through the woods as a wolf.

And that was if she didn't run from me screaming when she finally saw my wolf. It would be quite a different vision to that of Jay's wolf. The silver shifter animal I became could scare a full-sized bear.

We walked down the steps of our home and along the road toward my parents' place.

"Mom and Dad's home is ten houses down." I pointed to show her where we were headed, as we walked along the path.

Our small pack town was made up of four long streets surrounding a central set of shops, and the town center where we all convened for social events and meetings. The town was surrounded by woodlands, hence our name, and the pack territory extended well into the forest, giving us all plenty of room to run whenever we needed it.

Men started to appear from nowhere as we walked, as if drawn by the unusual scent of a young female. The Alpha in me grabbed Claire around the waist and hauled her into my side.

We hadn't had a woman under fifty in our town in years. No one brought the city women home. It was an unwritten rule.

Two young shifters from another mini-triad pack, Thomas and Grady, stood on their balcony, gaping at us as we walked past.

Grady called out. "Dexter, who you got there?"

Claire pushed at me, wriggling in my tight grip. "Can you ease up? You're going to break one of my ribs if you're not careful."

I immediately let her go and waved at Grady, unwilling to answer his question by shouting it out across the street.

"Yeah, sorry," I said instead to Claire.

She continued next to me, not moving too far away. "Why are they all looking at me as if I'm dinner? Oh God... you weren't exaggerating, were you? The town really is all men, isn't it?"

I laughed without humor. "Did you think we were lying about that?"

"Um... no. But you've got to admit, it's unusual. I've never seen anything like it."

Pack members were emerging from every direction, across the square and out of the shops. They must all have been able to smell her.

I knew I could. And it was making my balls ache and my skin tingle.

My mate was here! She was within touching distance, and I had to tamp down on my need and lust, and not take her in the street like my savage side demanded.

I wanted them all to know, to see that we'd found her. And I wanted to stamp my claim on her, in front of everyone.

She was *mine*.

Correction.

She was mine, Taylor's and Jay's. My pack.

Ours...

"There she is." I pointed to my mother, who stood on the steps outside her huge home, watching us make our way toward her.

She'd raised my three brothers and me in that house. It now seemed empty without us. Or so she said. To me it still felt like coming home, when I visited.

Claire walked ahead of me up the path and my mother welcomed her with open arms.

Claire embraced my mom and they walked inside with their arms wrapped around each other, as if they'd known one another their entire lives.

My heart thumped weirdly and a grin lifted my lips. I looked over at Taylor. "What's with that?"

He shrugged. "I don't know. Some sort of woman thing?"

I didn't know either, so I continued up the path and into the house. I could hear them talking from the kitchen. For the first time ever, I felt like an outsider in my own home.

Jay and Taylor quickly followed me inside, and the three of us piled into the kitchen and stood by the table, listening as Claire informed my mother of my father's condition.

"Will he be all right?" Mom asked, with a worried look etching her features.

Claire didn't answer straight away. But then she reached over and touched my mother's hand with hers.

"Honestly, I don't know. If he was just a normal man, I'd say his chances of surviving a year to be about fifty per cent."

My mother inhaled sharply. That was not the news she wanted to hear.

Claire continued. "But he isn't human, so I'm not sure I can give you a full answer. I'm assuming wolf shifters have increased healing, or some other abilities that I don't know about? Is that correct?"

She looked around the room and I nodded.

"Yeah, as shifters, we heal very rapidly. Damage to the heart is a bit different, but with the operation, I think my father should recover much faster than any other man his age."

Claire nodded and my mother fixed me with a stare. "Dexter, how about you go speak to Bill about what you've found out today? I'll keep Claire company."

The tone of my mother's voice was clear. She wanted me to leave.

But, why? And what if someone else came by and saw Claire? Could I trust the rest of the pack not to touch my mate?

"Mom, I don't think that's a good idea."

Claire turned in her chair and looked at me. For the first time I read understanding in her gaze. Did she know my protective streak was all for her? I couldn't help myself; I just wanted to ensure she was safe. And in time, happy.

"It's fine, Dexter," she said firmly. "I'm sure your mom can look after me as well as you men can."

I doubted that very much, but wasn't about to say that in front of my mother.

"I suppose Bill will be interested in what we've learnt about human mates," I managed. The elder was one of those who had split us younger men up into mini-packs of three. Bill would most definitely be interested in what we'd discovered about Claire being the mate of all three of us, but it was difficult at this early stage to consider leaving her in someone else's care, even for a short time.

I'd been brought up to be as selfless as possible. To believe the good of the pack was the most important thing, and to rise above selfish endeavors. And I stood by that ethos ninety-nine per cent of the time. This moment seemed to be the other one per cent.

"Come on Dexter. Let's go. The girls wanna talk." Jay tugged at my arm, and with a final huff, I let my Omega pull me away.

"Okay. Well, um..." I trailed off. Claire was already accepting a cup of tea from my mother and falling into conversation the way only women could do.

I turned away, fighting my wolf the whole time. He didn't want to leave his mate, and I felt the exact same way.

But once we trotted down the stairs and got back into the fresh air, the tortured feeling of being dragged away from her finally lifted a little.

And I could breathe again.

And then I remembered what Jay had been doing when Taylor and I walked into the lounge room.

I pushed him in the shoulder, hard, and he staggered sideways.

"Hey! What was that for?" he grumbled, shooting me a glare.

"For being the first one to kiss our mate... twice! And if we hadn't walked in when we did, you would have seduced her right out from under us."

Instead of denying anything, my Omega grinned. "What can I say? For the first time in my life, I'm actually enjoying being the smallest of our pack. She finds me the least intimidating."

I had to give him that. Jay had always hated that he couldn't hold his own the way Taylor and I could in a fight. He was the smallest, the slowest, and the most likely to get hurt if ever the bear shifters attacked.

No wonder Claire felt most comfortable with him first. He was the closest thing to a human we had.

"Yeah, well don't think you'll be the last, because I'm dying to taste her," I muttered.

Taylor grunted. "Me, too. So, what are we going to tell Bill and the other elders?"

I shrugged and kept walking, nodding to people as I went.

"I don't know. I suppose we have to be honest about imprinting on a human. After all, it may be the way to save the entire pack. If our triad did it, maybe some of the others will be able to, as well."

Jay nodded. "Yeah, I think it is a way to save our pack. New blood. New wolves when the children arrive. A way for the pack to grow and maybe even thrive in new and different ways. Ways we don't even know about, yet."

We made our way to Bill's house and regaled the astonished elder with our tale of finding Claire at the hospital, and her fainting spells when we touched her.

The old man's eyes lit up like the fourth of July. I'd thought he might be disappointed that humans were the answer to our problem, but clearly, he wasn't.

He shook our hands and thanked us. I think he even had the glint of a tear in his eye when he did so.

It seemed that, in finding Claire, we may very well have saved our whole pack from extinction.

8

CLAIRE

"Mary, I just don't know what to think about all this," I said to Dexter's mother. "I'm sorry. I know you've grown up with it... I mean, you *are* one, I guess. But wolf shifters! Honestly... I feel like I'm stuck in some vampire movie on the T.V."

Mary Monaghan, Dexter's mother, laughed good naturedly. As soon as she had welcomed me in with a hug, I had felt calm and safe. As if I had found my way to the very place I needed to be.

"Well, sweetie, unfortunately I have to tell you that I think you're the strange one. Why wouldn't you turn into a powerful wolf at will, if you could?"

She grinned at me and I rolled my eyes and laughed with her.

She was right, of course. Everyone's version of normal was exactly that. *Their* version of what they saw and became used to every day in their own lives. Who was I to claim that I was the normal one in this situation?

I rubbed my eyes, still feeling a little like I had fallen down the proverbial rabbit hole.

"How do you feel about mating with all three of them?" Mary suddenly asked me, and I almost spat out my mouthful of tea.

I swallowed hard and then gasped for air, fanning my face to try and cool my suddenly hot cheeks. "How did you know about that? Oh, they told you."

Seriously, they were worse than gossiping women.

Mary laughed again. "It's nothing to be ashamed of. They're proud to have you as their mate—if you'll accept them, that is. But I do have to tell you that the threesome thing is new and different, even for us. Usually, or at least how it worked in the past, our mates and families are one-to-one. But then again, we've never had to make the boys group up into triads before. So maybe that's how it happened."

I cocked my head and concentrated on what she was saying. This could be important. "What do you mean?"

"Well, in the past, say when I was younger, most of us had mated by twenty-one. There were enough women for all the men. People rarely left the pack and we were a big enough lot to avoid too much cousin cross-breeding, or anything like that."

I couldn't stop the shudder that ran through my body. "Was that beginning to happen, though? Too much of the same bloodlines?"

Mary's face twisted up a little as though she was thinking hard. "I... suppose. You know, I've never really thought about it, but you're probably right. The actual true mate's legend was becoming less frequent and some people were pairing up with cousins only because there was no one left to mate with."

That often happened with small, isolated communities like this one.

It was unfortunate, but nature usually found a way around it.

"And the next generation—*your* generation—bore only males?" I asked, confirming what had been said by Jay.

"Yes. Not a single female has been born in almost fifty years. I bore my husband four sons, and the rest of the pack contributed thirty-five boys."

"And that's why you made them group up into threes?" I re-iterated. I wanted to get this right.

"Well, yes. There was going to be too much infighting, otherwise. Too many Alphas like Dexter, who couldn't mate. The hormones, the anger, the frustration. It could have led to the downfall of our pack."

I still had some questions. "So why three, then?"

I could see there were differences between Jay, Taylor and Dexter, but I really couldn't work out exactly what the balance was.

"An Alpha, a Beta and an Omega. The perfect triad of men," Mary told me, in a tone that indicated she assumed I knew what she was saying.

"Ah…" I didn't really want to ask her to explain again, but I had no real idea what those terms meant. I could figure out that an Alpha was a strong leader, and I could see those traits in Dexter. But the other terms… My confusion must have shown in my expression, because Mary sighed.

"An Alpha is a leader, the strongest and the biggest of the wolves. A Beta is close behind him. Slightly smaller in stature, he is an Alpha's right-hand man. An Omega is the smallest of our family, but the sweetest and most family-oriented of all."

"So…" This was easy. "Dexter's the Alpha, Taylor's the Beta and Jay's the Omega."

Mary nodded. "Yes, it's pretty easy to figure out once you see them all together."

"Okay, I'm understanding why you put them into families, but what does that have to do with me?"

Mary grinned. "You get the best of all worlds. I married an Alpha, see, and he is beautiful, but he is a little standoffish and can often put the needs of the pack above mine. More often than not, actually." She sighed and took a sip of tea. "But if you have all three men, you'll always be taken care of. You'll never be alone. All your physical and emotional needs will be taken care of. When one slacks off a little, one of the others will step up. You will get all the protection and strength and love and compassion you ever need. If I had my time over again, I'd jump at the chance to add a Beta and an Omega into the mix with my husband." She ducked her head, as if slightly embarrassed by her own words. "Even though he *is* my soul mate."

My mind went blank, in the strangest way. Like it had been blown apart and I could consider nothing other than the extreme amount of information that I didn't know, about this world.

Could it be possible?

"Do you, um, have a job, Mary? A career? How does that fit into this scenario?" I loved being a doctor. I didn't think I'd ever be able to give up healing. Not even for a soul mate—or three.

Mary shook her head. "I'm a homemaker, Claire, but honestly, that's by choice. All I ever wanted was to be married and raise my boys right. I never had a career like you, as a doctor. But I never wanted one."

"Do you think..." I couldn't believe where my thoughts were taking me. This was crazy. To even consider...

"If you're asking if you could still be a doctor, if you take on my son and his pack, I'd say you need to ask them that question. But with three of them there—including one Omega who loves looking after children..." She shrugged, and my mind reeled at the sudden possibilities.

"I hadn't thought of it like that."

I'd always been amazed by the flaws in a one-to-one ratio of women to men. I didn't know a single woman who was fully satisfied by her husband.

There was always something lacking. Sex, or friendship, or help around the house.

Every one of my married friends complained about their husbands in some way.

They didn't help with the kids.

They didn't make enough money.

There was no emotional support.

No sex.

Too much sex.

The lists were always endless, and for me, I always agreed with them. The few boyfriends I'd had were shallow creeps. No one even came close to fulfilling the emotional needs of my heart, let alone the physical needs of my body.

Was it really possible that this was what I needed? Three men? And wolf shifters, at that.

Because I knew that solitary human males had failed every task I'd ever set.

"Thanks for the chat, Mary. It looks like I have a lot of thinking to do."

Mary pushed a homemade cookie at me and smiled. "You do that. And no pressure or anything, but I would love to have you as a daughter-in-law. After four sons, I crave female company more than anything. As soon as I saw you, I felt a kinship connection."

Tears sprang to my eyes, though there was nothing to cry about. But Mary's words were so heartfelt I had to walk around the kitchen counter and hug her. How could I not?

She laughed as I held her. Then I remembered the other reason we'd come over.

"Oh, Mary. Is there any way I could borrow some clothes for a few days? Looks like I'm sticking around and I don't think the boys want to drive me home at the moment to grab some of my own things."

I had so many clothes at home it was embarrassing. The fact that I had to ask to borrow some felt ridiculous.

Mary laughed and dragged me into her bedroom. "Of course. Come this way."

We had a laugh and a chat as we found some jeans, tanks, shoes, and even a serviceable black dress for me to wear. Just until I went home, of course.

When we were done, Mary offered to walk me back to Dexter's house, and I accepted straight away. I didn't want to face the walk on my own, with all of those men looking at me again.

As we walked, I was glad the older woman was with me. The

number of eyes on us was incredible. It was one of the most intimidating things I'd ever experienced, and I'd lectured at university before! But nothing in my past life came close to the feeling of dozens of male eyes on me. Assessing the way I looked, the way I walked. Quite possibly sizing me up as a possible mate.

But I wasn't their mate. Not at all. There was no pull toward any of them, like there had been with Dexter, Taylor and Jay.

Every one of the men was young and fit and had more muscles than I could count.

"Is everyone in this town a body builder?" I asked as we got closer to Dexter's house.

My heart was pounding in my chest and it took all of my self-control to keep walking at a slow pace, and not bolt for the front door. My arms and legs tingled with adrenaline. I wanted to run!

Mary smiled. "This is a shifter pack, hun. All the men are fit and strong. Some of the elders are getting a bit soft around the middle, but the wolf genes even keep them pretty fit."

I glanced over at Mary. She walked like a woman my age. With grace and strength and poise. She was slightly more fleshy than was currently fashionable, like me, but I could see the latent strength behind the curves.

"Thank you so much for helping me today, Mary. I really appreciate the insight."

She hugged me tightly and kissed my cheek, the sweet scent of her warmth washing over me.

"I know it must be hard for you, but try to be patient with them, okay?"

I nodded and watched her walk away. Two men stepped off their porch and began to walk toward me. I squealed as I ran inside, locking the front door behind me.

Fuck. That was intense.

I felt like *Alice in Wonderland,* because I had seriously fallen down a rabbit hole.

When was I going to wake up?

I wandered around the living area, the room much cleaner than I'd have expected with three men living in the house.

But where were the photos, the personal effects? I glanced toward the stairs. Their rooms, perhaps?

I shook my head and laughed at myself a little. I couldn't possibly... could I? I mean... would it be that bad if I had a little look around their rooms? I had to know something about these men. They seemed to know me.

My hand was on the rail and my feet were walking up the stairs to the bedrooms before I even finished making the decision to do so.

It was wrong to go snooping.

But so was kidnapping an unconscious woman from a hospital.

I giggled to myself. "This is merely touché."

The first room on the right was dark and, as I flipped on the light, my eyes bulged at the sexiness of the room. I was scared to move closer to the bed in case a sex swing dropped from the ceiling, or something.

I wasn't sure if it was Taylor's room, or Dexter's, but the details screamed *Alpha*.

Dexter's, I decided, studying the strong, confident space. The size of the massive wooden furniture. The silver sheets and mirrors that would match the colors of Dexter's wolf, or so they'd said.

There was something super sexy in the energy of this bedroom and the bed looked so comfortable, with massive pillows and a duvet just calling to my tired body.

I crept in and looked around the room, wanting details about these men. Dexter, in particular.

There was nothing too defining. No photos or memorabilia of any kind.

Did these wolves live minimalist lifestyles on purpose? Or was this the result of a lack of feminine touch?

"See anything you like?" Dexter purred from the doorway and I jumped and swiveled around.

"Oh, shit! You scared me." I put a hand to my chest, feeling my heart hammering away.

Heat flushed my face, mostly from being caught with my hand in the cookie jar.

But if I were honest, there was another reason my cheeks were hot—the intense desire that wove through my body whenever Dexter was present.

He leaned against the door with the casual confidence of a fifties movie star.

His jeans hung on his lean hips like they were ready to fall to the ground any moment and his shoulders barely fit through the door, he was so huge.

"Ah... I'm guessing this is your room? I wasn't sure, but it felt like it for some reason."

He began to stalk forward and I couldn't stop the way my throat tightened and my belly clenched.

Damn, he was so sexy.

I wanted him. More than I'd ever wanted anyone in my life. But dare I go after what my body so desperately craved?

He kept prowling forward and I backed up, until my legs buckled against the bed and I landed on my ass on the mattress.

He kept advancing over me and I shuffled up onto the bed.

He slid right over the top of me and I found myself staring up at the hottest man to ever rise above me.

9

CLAIRE

He didn't kiss me though, as I had expected. Instead, he stared down at me, a muscle tightening and ticking in his jaw as though he fought our attraction with every breath he took.

That gave me the strangest sense of power, knowing he wanted me that much and yet would fight to give me the choice.

"Aren't you going to kiss me?" I managed to ask, though my chest was tight with expectation and I was literally squirming on the bed from the ache between my thighs.

He frowned a little, lines forming between his eyebrows. "You said I was the scariest of all."

I wanted to laugh. I wanted to run. But more than anything I wanted to grab him and pull him down on top of me, just to feel the sheer weight of his body on mine.

"You are," I admitted, and he began to move away, retreating from the bed, disappointment etched on his face.

I grabbed his arms and held him still. I didn't want him to go anywhere. "You didn't let me finish."

He slowly moved back above me, so he could look straight into my eyes once again.

"What else is there, Claire?"

I reached up and ran my hands slowly over his arms, the huge muscles bulging and flexing beneath my fingers.

I could feel the animal attraction between us as though it were a solid object. It burned and flickered like a flame, but not intense enough to knock me out again. *Thank God.* It was more muted now, but somehow stronger, because I was awake and could experience the full effect.

"You're scary because you're so strong. You could tear me apart with these muscles... couldn't you, Dexter?"

He clenched his jaw. "I'd never hurt you."

I arched my back, unable to stay away from him. I wanted to be naked, to feel him against my flesh.

God, I am such a wanton at the moment!

What have these men done to me?

"I know... but can't you see how scary that is for me? To know you could hurt me, yet needing to trust you to protect me instead."

Dexter groaned and dropped his weight down on top of mine.

My legs opened of their own accord and he settled between my thighs like it was the most natural thing in the world.

Then, suddenly, he flipped us and I was on top, looking down on the massive man.

"You have all the power, Claire. As my mate, a woman I've waited my whole life for, I'd die to keep you safe."

I sucked in a breath. The intensity of what he was saying was truly mind-blowing.

In my world, men didn't say such things, especially to women they'd just met.

I pushed the fear from my mind and slipped my hands beneath Dexter's tank top. His skin sizzled beneath my palms and I gasped at the way my core melted, arousal weaving through every cell of my body.

I stroked along his rock-hard abs, finding his erect nipples with my fingertips. Torturing both of us until all I could feel was an insatiable need to have him fill me.

And what was stopping me?

I hadn't been with anyone in months. More than months. It felt like forever. And I had three gorgeous men willing to fulfil every fantasy I'd ever had.

What was I doing... trying to run away from them?

I only had two days to decide whether to stay or go. What was I waiting for?

I lowered my body down on top of him and pressed my lips to Dexter's mouth.

He groaned against me and flipped us so he was once again on top.

I wanted to cry out with glee at how right it felt to have my arms and legs wrapped around Dexter's body, to have his mouth on mine.

My mind was whirling with pleasure, my body singing in rapture.

I pulled at his top, needing to get closer.

He rolled to the side and threw the shirt across the room.

I sat up and lifted my arms. My scrubs and old bra ended up on the floor beside me.

In the back of my mind, I knew I wanted Taylor and Jay here too. I missed them in a strange way. But I was too desperate. Something innate was driving me to bond with Dexter first. Was it the Alpha thing they'd all talked about?

I didn't really know, and I didn't care at this point in time.

Dexter tugged at my shoes and my pants, then my underwear was gone too, in a flurry of moaning and laughing and kissing.

His jeans disappeared like they'd never been there, and suddenly he was back on top of me.

I would have liked to take my time exploring him, gazing at the wonder of his body. But my need was too great. I could read equal desire in his hungry gaze as he stared down at me, and I knew we wouldn't be taking our time.

I gripped his shoulders, unwilling to let him go for a moment.

I ground my pelvis against his and he leaned back a little, putting space between us so he could test my arousal with his fingers.

I gasped and he groaned as he rubbed around my swollen clit with his fingers, spreading my wetness and then sliding a single digit into my aching core.

I cried out and shuddered at the invasion.

I needed so much more than just one finger. I ached so badly for his solid hard flesh. I needed him properly seated inside me.

"You're very wet." His tone was full of wonder, and perhaps surprise.

"I am. Please..." I couldn't say anything else coherent, so I pulled at his arms to get him back on top of me again. Close, like I needed.

Dexter slid down, the head of his cock lining up at my entrance.

I could feel the rigid flesh butting against my entrance.

And then he was taking me, sliding in to the hilt. I cried out, gasping at his thickness. The length. The strange pain and possession I felt pulsing through me as we finally connected in this way.

I'd never felt anything like it. So perfect. So right. "Oh my God," I whispered, digging my nails into his arms and arching my back, trying to get comfortable enough to take all of him.

"Fuck... you're so tight." So was his voice. He sounded as if he were holding onto control by his fingertips.

I nodded. I knew I would be.

He waited and I panted, struggling to get comfortable around the invasion.

Then the throbbing began again, the need and the want building in me.

"Please," I repeated again, digging my teeth into the top of his shoulder and clenching hard with my internal muscles around him.

He groaned loudly, the animalistic noise vibrating right through to my core.

He pulled almost all the way out, then thrust back in. I cried out at the amazing sensation and wound my legs around his waist. Wanting more.

He did it again and again, torturing us both with the too-slow speed. But then he began to move faster and harder.

My cries became louder as he thrust into my needy body and I had no control over them. I heard them from a distance, like it wasn't even me making those crazy sounds.

I was a bundle of energy, of screaming nerve endings and lust.

The tension in my belly was building higher and tighter and as I began to climax, I called out to him, wanting to bring him with me over the edge.

"Oh... *Dex!*"

He slammed his cock into me again and again, the wooden headboard banging against the wall until I cried out in the ultimate pleasure.

My orgasm swept me up and for several moments, I didn't exist. I was floating beyond the plane of existence... and then I was falling back into my body, which was screaming and shuddering and rippling around Dexter's thick cock.

He fell on me, grabbing my ass in both hands and burying himself deeply inside me one last time.

Then he began to come.

Torrents of heat pulsed into my body and I cried out as another, smaller orgasm hit me, squeezing in time with Dexter's squirting cock.

And then it was over and we both lay panting, gripping each other in the aftermath of what had to be the hottest session I'd ever experienced.

Dexter rolled us until he was on his back and I was laying on his chest, struggling to catch my breath and loving the sound of his racing heart beneath my ear.

I looked over my shoulder, half expecting to see Jay or Taylor there in the doorway, watching us. But there was no one except Dex and me in the room.

However, there was still a feeling of their absence. Dex was amazing, but I wanted Taylor and Jay there, too.

"You are incredible," Dexter groaned out, kissing the top of my head.

I laughed at the unfamiliar compliment. What else could I do? I'd been told previously I was boring in bed. I had never expected to hear any man say I was incredible, especially when it came to sex.

"Um... thanks. But you're the incredible one. Is that the mating thing you were talking about?"

He rubbed my back, his hand moving up and down my spine in a soothing rhythm I could get very used to.

"It's the start of it. Yes. But there's so much more to it than that. Sleep, beautiful."

"Oh... I'll just rest for a bit."

I didn't mean to fall asleep, and normally I never would.

Not after sex.

But the sense of peace and safety I felt when I was lying in Dexter's arms, was beautiful, and I didn't stop myself as my body relaxed against the pillows.

TAYLOR

The banging and screaming and noises of vigorous sex coming from Dexter's room had finally stopped, but the anger in my gut continued to stew.

"He's got her in his bed, upstairs. He's taken her, already, before us."

"Yeah, so?" Jay called from the kitchen. "He is the Alpha. It's how it should be."

Jay might have been right, in a sense, but I couldn't stay still. My feet shuffled and shifted, unable to stay still, and my heart raced like I'd been running through the woods.

"So… should we go up there? Should we join them?"

Jay and I looked at each other, considering my suggestion. Should we? Then it was too late. I heard a door open, then close, and Dexter's heavy tread on the stairs.

I turned and leaned against the kitchen counter, feigning nonchalance. It wouldn't help anyone if Dex knew how jealous I was that he'd gotten to Claire first.

Dexter bounced down the bottom two stairs, his jeans hanging off his hips, the buttons haphazardly done up.

His smile was lazy, his other clothes were all missing, and I was pretty sure I could spy bite marks on his shoulder.

Bite marks!

I crossed my arms over my chest and struggled against the swirl of emotions whittling away at my gut. I could not be jealous of a member of my own pack. I couldn't. Especially not the Alpha. We'd never survive sharing a mate if this was how it felt every time Claire had sex with one of the other two.

Especially when I'd been the one to point out how many benefits this would bring for all of us, if we decided to embrace her as our mate for the whole mini-pack.

But it was a losing battle inside my own mind.

"How was she?" I bit out, unable to control myself. My tone was vile—even I could hear that—and Dexter gave me a reproving look.

"What's up with you?"

I uncrossed my arms and began to pace the kitchen. Back and forth. Vibrating with rage. How could he ask that? How could he *not* know... "I don't know. I feel... fuck... I don't know. Restless, angry. Like I want to punch something, or run."

I was full of testosterone. And I damn sure needed either a fight, or a good fuck.

Dexter laughed, and I nearly jumped over the countertop and launched myself at him. In that moment, I was prouder of my self-control than I've ever been in my life.

"That's just because you haven't mated with her yet," Dex said. "When she wakes up, go get her. She was looking for you and Jay during our session. I could sense it."

She was? His words calmed me, a tiny bit, at least.

"You felt like this earlier too?"

Dexter nodded as he moved across the kitchen and pulled out a plate of leftovers from the fridge.

"Oh, yeah. I was ready to rip Jay's head off for kissing her first, but now I feel... I don't know... happy. Settled. Whereas before, I thought my wolf might jump forth and shift without permission."

"That's exactly how I feel!"

He was telling me that relief was in sight? I glanced at the stairs. How long would it take until she woke up? And once she did, could I even guarantee that she'd still want me? Maybe Dexter had given her everything she needed, and the spark of attraction between her and me would be gone.

My teeth clenched at the thought. No. I wouldn't consider that option. I couldn't bear it, if that were the case.

"So, is this how we're gonna do things? Have her one at a time?" Jay asked, and we both turned to look at him.

"Ah... I suppose. Why?" I glanced at Dexter, considering what he'd said a minute or two earlier. *She was looking for you and Jay.* Then he shrugged. This was new to all of us.

Jay pulled more groceries from the refrigerator and began chopping fruit. "I don't know. I kinda thought that working on her together would be fun."

I caught Dexter's surprised expression and grinned at him. Our Omega wanted to work Claire's body *with* us?

I'd always thought Jay's testosterone was lacking. Clearly not. Obviously, he had simply needed the presence of his mate to bring out that aspect in him.

"Well, let's see what she says when she wakes up. Because no matter what, we need to get to know her individually, I think. We're still separate people."

One pack, yes.

But we were all very different, and Claire needed to know what she was getting herself into, one at a time, instead of as a package deal.

"I made a deal with Claire to get her to stay," Jay said suddenly, and we turned toward him.

"What did you offer her?" I asked, dread tingling on the ends of my nerves.

Jay bit his lip, a sure sign he'd done something wrong. "I told her that we'd drive her home again if she wanted us to."

"You what?" Dexter and I practically yelled at him.

Jay backed away, his hands held up in a sign of peace. "It was all I could think of. What else was I going to say when she was so afraid? And look what's happened already... Dexter mated with her."

I ran a hand through my hair, my arm vibrating with anger. "You told her she could *leave*?"

I wanted to wring his neck.

"I told her to stay for two days so that we had time to *convince* her to stay. She's giving us a chance, and that's thanks to me."

Jay glared at me and I glared back, and that's when I heard a soft sigh and tentative footsteps coming down the stairs.

"We'll deal with this later," I hissed at Jay, and turned around to see Claire gingerly stepping down the last few steps.

She'd put her scrubs back on but they were in pretty bad shape.

"Um... I was going to have a nap, but thought I'd ask if I can have a quick shower first?"

Her eyes were half asleep and there was a lack of tension in her body that I hadn't even realized was there initially.

"You look really relaxed," I couldn't help saying, even though the words came out of me begrudgingly, and the heat of a blush spread straight up her face.

"Oh... well..."

I could see by her expression she wanted to say more, but we didn't know each other well enough yet. And I needed to change that, but I wasn't sure how to start. Grabbing her and dragging her up to my bedroom so I could mate with her, too, didn't seem like the right way to woo her.

Maybe Jay was right, and we did need more time.

"Oh, sorry! I'll show you where the shower is and then if you're up for it, we can go for a walk or something, if you want. I can show you more of the town."

Claire nodded and grabbed the clothes off the couch before following me into the main downstairs bathroom.

"Here you go." I pointed to the stack of clean towels on a shelf in the bathroom, and then backed out to leave her alone.

She retreated quickly, shutting the door behind her.

I returned to the kitchen, feeling even more needy than I had before. Now all I could imagine was Claire's naked body under the cascading shower water. I felt like I was about to burst out of my skin.

Dexter laughed, as if sensing my frustration, and slapped me on the back. "Way to make her feel comfortable."

It was too much. I wanted to punch him in the face and he must have seen it, because he backed away quickly.

"Well, I'd better get over to work for a while, since I feel like I could seriously lift a building and... you look like you want to demolish one. Good luck, Taylor."

Dexter headed upstairs, presumably to grab some clothes, and I sat down with a plate of food in front of me and shoveled in as much as I could.

The feelings of anger and need inside me were building to epic proportions, and I wasn't sure how to settle them.

Claire emerged from the bathroom a few minutes later, her pretty face flushed pink from the hot water, dressed in some worn jeans and a white t-shirt.

"You look gorgeous," I managed, through my thick tongue. She looked good enough to eat. Literally.

"You hungry?" Jay asked her, and pushed a sandwich on a plate across the bench.

She pulled up a stool and sat. "Yeah, a bit. Thanks."

She tucked into the meal and Jay put everything else away, his movements sharp and jerky in a way they hadn't been before.

When he walked into his room and shut the door, I couldn't help but feel sorry for the guy. He needed to wait until I'd mated with her, and then it would be his turn. If I were him, I wouldn't want to wait, and he was obviously struggling as much as me.

"Do you want to check out the town?" I asked Claire. "Or is there anything else you'd like to do today?"

I could see her swaying on her feet. "Um... actually I'd love a proper nap, if there's somewhere I can sleep? I was at the end of a sixteen-hour shift this morning and I'm feeling lethargic."

A good orgasm will do that to you.

I looked toward Jay's room, where the door was firmly shut.

"Well... Jay is using his room, and I'm gonna assume Dexter's room is a mess, so you can sleep in my bed if you want, but I've gotta warn you, it's pretty male. Nothing too friendly and frilly."

She laughed. "Have you seen Dexter's room? It can't be worse than that."

I shrugged and pointed to the stairs.

In some ways it probably *was* worse than Dexter's room. Not warm or masculine, it was hot and modern.

She took to the stairs in front of me and I watched her ass swing as she walked.

Fuck.

Shouldn't have done that. I looked away, trying to control my lustful thoughts.

Now my cock was swelling and I wanted to knock her to the ground and mount her right there in the hallway.

I forced myself to slow my steps and watched her walk ahead. I gulped in deep breaths of the air around me, trying in vain to slow the beating of my heart. My hands clenched at my sides as I struggled with my own base instincts.

This was *insane.*

If I were a true animal, this had to be what it felt like to be around a female in heat.

When she turned back with a query on her face, I gulped and pointed ahead. "That's it, first door after the bathroom, on your left."

She turned into my bedroom and I could hear her gasp from where I stood.

It didn't scare me—instead that gasp made me ache for her even more. Ache to hear those sounds in my ear as she rode my cock.

"I told you," I said as I walked into my room behind her. "It's pretty different to Dexter's space."

My room was red and black. Harsh and dynamic colors, with steel furniture and hard edges.

"I love it. It's very... sexy." She moved over to the curtains and drew them shut.

Darkness enveloped us and she began to undress.

I could hear movement in the dark and my chest began to tighten and ache. I needed to get out of here, before I lost control completely.

"I'll let you sleep."

I turned to move away and heard her deep sigh.

It stopped me. I wasn't sure how I knew, but I could sense she wanted to say something.

"Is something wrong, Claire?" I asked, turning to face her slowly.

"I don't know how to do this. I'm so awkward."

Despite the desire raging through me, I laughed. "You are the opposite of awkward. You're sexy, sensual and beautiful. Not awkward at all. If anything, I'm the one feeling awkward right now."

I couldn't see the smile on her face in the darkness, but I hoped it was there. I wanted to make her happy.

"Okay..." She pulled back the covers and climbed in, but there was something else she wanted to say. I could feel it.

"Whatever it is, Claire, you can tell me."

Did she want to mate with Dexter alone, and not have anything to do with us? That would be my worst nightmare come true, but what else would make her hesitate like that? She must be able to sense how much I wanted her. And if she didn't want me in return...

"Would you stay with me for a while? Just, you know... to cuddle."

Hell, yes. "Of course, I will."

I was out of my clothes and under the covers in seconds.

I lay on my back on the pillows and Claire crawled over to me, laying her head on my shoulder and her hand over my racing heart.

My wolf was going crazy inside me.

I had no idea how I was going to lay here and let her sleep, but I had to. If she wanted to cuddle, then she'd get a cuddle.

I should be grateful she wanted me at all, even for a cuddle, after being with Dexter. The Alpha, after all, did have the best traits of a pack mate.

Her hand began to stroke my chest in a soothing, soft way.

"Are you naked?" she asked suddenly.

"Um... yeah. I sleep naked."

This was normal behavior for me. We didn't even bother with underwear. What was the point when you were shifting every other day?

"Oh... okay..."

She cuddled in closer and her heat began to envelop me. A scent I'd never before smelt caught my nose.

Was it Dexter's seed? No... she'd had a shower. Then what was it?

I inhaled again. My cock filled with blood. *Oh, damn.* That was desire I smelt. *Her* desire. She wanted me.

"Taylor?" Claire's voice was soft, but I knew she could feel the blanket shifting as my cock rose.

"I'm sorry. I have no control over that whatsoever."

"Oh... it's not a bad thing... I just wasn't sure... after Dexter... if you wanted me or not."

"Wanted you? Are you kidding me?"

I grabbed her hand and pushed it down my body, letting her feel my hard-on.

"This doesn't lie, sweetheart."

She gasped as her hand touched my flesh, then she wrapped her palm around the shaft and I let my hand drop away.

She wasn't moving and my cock throbbed with blood. It was getting thicker and harder by the minute.

"Um... Can I...?"

"Sweetheart, you can do anything you want." My voice was gruff with need.

She lowered her head and wet heat engulfed the head of my shaft as her mouth took me in.

"Holy shit." I bucked my hips up, unable to stop the reaction, shoving myself deep into Claire's mouth.

She moaned, but didn't stop, sucking and moving her sweet lips and tongue up and down my cock.

I clenched the sheets either side of me, not wanting to grab her head and force her down on me.

But, God did I want to.

She went up on her knees next to me, and in that position she could take more into her mouth, and the smell of her arousal hit me like a truck.

Fuck this.

I twisted and grabbed her, lifting her up and placing her over my face, her legs on either side of my head and her pussy over my mouth.

"What are you..." she began to ask.

I pushed her underwear to the side and delved my tongue straight into her pussy.

She gasped and moaned, throwing her head back and forcing her body back onto my face.

I held her thighs wide and tongue fucked her over and over again, licking her clit and tasting her juices as they ran into my mouth.

"Taylor... Taylor!" Her voice was breathless, the sound of my name on her tongue like heaven in my ears.

"Come here." I growled out, pushing back the blankets and twisting her around so she was straddling me properly this time. "Take me in, beautiful."

Claire moved her underwear to the side and I grabbed my shaft, holding it up so she could ride it like a pole.

She slid up, found the head of my cock and impaled herself in one, smooth motion.

"Oh... fuck!" I wanted to yell at the perfect feel of her around me, but swallowed the sound down and let out a choked groan instead.

I'd never felt anything like it, and my wolf howled inside my mind at the completion of finally mating with *the one*.

Claire groaned and gasped as she slid up and down on me, her pussy rippling and gripping me with each descent.

I grabbed her hips, planted my feet onto the mattress and thrust up, fucking her as hard as I dared.

She moaned louder and held tight to my arms, bucking like a wild cowgirl atop a bucking bronco.

The pressure was building in my balls, the tightness in my gut growing as my pleasure soared.

"Taylor... Taylor... I'm... I'm going to..." Claire gasped and arched her back.

Her pussy began to wring me tightly, her rigid body obviously on the brink of climax.

I gave her everything I had, screaming out her name as my own orgasm swept me up, and pumped my seed deep into her core.

Claire cried out to me, her nails digging into my arms as she squeezed my cock tight and came all over me.

I held her to me, loving every last tremor that ran through her body as we found perfect bliss together.

My wolf finally calmed, my appetite quieted, and for the first time since we'd met Claire, I could think clearly.

Damn.

This must be what Dexter was talking about.

Claire had collapsed on top of me and seemed to have fallen asleep. Her breathing was slow and quiet and although I didn't want to wake her up, energy was leaping in my blood.

I couldn't lay down and stay still for the hours she might need to sleep.

I slowly rolled and shuffled her onto a pillow beside me. She half-woke a little but didn't speak, so I tucked her up in the duvet and slowly crept away.

I felt amazing!

As I stretched, I could feel new muscle growth, the sinew and tissues tighter and ready for anything coming our way.

Wow. Our parents had never said anything about this benefit when it came to mating.

I grabbed my clothes and crept out of the room, closing the door behind me so that Claire could sleep without being interrupted.

I didn't know much about the life of a physician, but she was obviously exhausted.

I pulled on my jeans as I walked down the hall and made my way down the stairs. Jay was sitting on the couch, determinedly looking at his phone and not me.

"Do I even want to know how it went?" he asked, not bothering to look up. "Wait, never mind. I heard it."

I grinned, happiness winging through my heart in a way I didn't understand.

"I'm heading out to work. See you for dinner."

I walked toward the front door and Jay called out. "What do you mean you're going to work? You seriously want to leave me here with her, after the two of you..."

I looked back at him, reading on his face the same discomfort that I'd been feeling earlier.

"Of course. You've gotta bond with her too, yeah? If I leave now, that'll give you some time alone to sort it out with her."

He nodded stiffly, and I wanted to tell him that relief was around the corner, if Claire was up for three in a day. That's probably why Dexter kept grinning at me earlier. He knew what was coming, and I had the feeling Jay would soon find out, too. But I didn't say anything further at this point. He wouldn't believe me, anyway.

Let him find out for himself.

I left the house whistling, the sun shining on my face. I closed my eyes for a few seconds and just breathed in the fresh air.

Life was sweet, and with our fated mate in our lives, it would only get sweeter.

11

———

JAY

What the hell was I going to do during the hours between now and dinner?

I glanced at the clock on the wall and relief swept through my body.

Okay... so that wasn't too bad. It was only three hours until Dexter and Taylor returned. Maybe Claire would sleep the whole time? And then what? I'd have to wait until tomorrow to hold her, kiss her. Love her the way Dexter and Taylor already had.

I tore at my hair on either side of my head, pulling hard to generate the pain I needed to push at the tension inside my body. I needed to shift and run. I needed... something.

The others now seemed so relaxed and carefree, while I wanted to pick up the fridge and throw it through the kitchen window. No prizes for guessing why.

My arms shook with the strain of holding in the need. And I couldn't even fully explain what it was, or why it was there.

I let loose a growl, my throat vibrating with the tension.

May as well get busy, and do something constructive with all this nervous energy and tension.

I put dinner on, cleaned the house and worked out in our home gym, pushing way past my normal barriers and lifting weights I'd never even contemplated before.

By the time the Dex and Taylor came home, I was covered in sweat and the whole house smelled like roasting lamb.

"Whoa, you went all out for Claire, huh?" Dexter said as he walked in the door, a big smile on his stupidly happy face.

I didn't know how to deal with all that happiness. "I need a shower," I said gruffly. "You guys dish up and I'll go check on her."

"Oh, she didn't wake up while we were gone?" Taylor asked, and shot a knowing look at Dex.

Great. Now the two of them would probably begin to pity me.

I shook my head and trotted up the stairs, deciding to check on Claire before the shower. As I left, I struggled to even look at my pack mates while they grinned at each other and then at me, like hyenas.

Obviously, mating with Claire had made them feel great. Sex would do that, I supposed. But this was different somehow. They seemed... really happy. More so than a simple act of sex would usually provide.

I trudged up the stairs and walked past Dexter's room.

The stench of sex was still there and I couldn't help but groan with frustration and longing as I walked toward Taylor's room.

This one would be even worse, I was sure. Fresher.

I knocked gently. "Claire?"

"Jay?"

I sighed. Yeah, I was going in. I cracked the door open a little and stuck my head in, the scent of sex pungent and hot as flames in my nostrils. It was like a slap in the face, to know what had just gone on in here, and without any involvement by me.

I sucked in a shallow breath and tried to speak while not breathing any deeper. "Dinner's ready whenever you are. I made roast lamb, if you like it?"

"Oh... great. I love roast, thank you. I won't be long."

I began to pull away. "Take your time. I'm gonna go have a shower. Meet you downstairs, okay?"

"Okay."

Her voice was quiet and as I shut the door, my heart ached.

Did she feel this? The need that actually hurt when it wasn't returned.

Probably not. She'd had Dexter and Taylor already today. Why would she feel the same needs I did?

It would be impossible.

I walked past the upstairs bathroom and paused in the hallway.

Maybe it was better to wash up here?

My shower, the one downstairs, would smell of Claire. She'd probably used my soap, one of my clean towels... I shuddered to think of the sensual torment such a thing would be like, to have a shower and be surrounded by her scent.

I stomped into the upstairs bathroom and shut the door. I needed a good, cold dunking more than anything else. I also stunk to high heaven, so a bloody good scrub was in order.

I flicked on the shower, stripped out of my clothes and jumped beneath the icy needles.

I yelped a bit when the water first hit my steaming skin, but sucked it up and dove beneath the fray. The cold water pummeled down on my head and I closed my eyes, splaying both hands onto the cold tiles and letting the water run down my back.

My heated skin began to shiver, and the frantic need within my muscles started to abate. A little.

Thank God for that.

I stood up straighter and turned the hot on, balancing out the temperature.

Slowly, the heat seeped into my bones and my muscles relaxed more fully. The steam began to rise around me and I took some deep, calming breaths.

That's better.

I turned my back on the head and grabbed the shampoo, pouring some of the liquid into my hands and scrubbing my hair with it.

My good stuff was downstairs, but this would have to do.

Taylor and Dexter would wash in the creek if I didn't insist on having soap and shampoo and showers in the house.

I was probably better suited to the human world than they were—and speaking of which...

The door to the bathroom slid open and a pair of dainty feet poked out beneath the steam.

Damn. I hadn't turned on the fan.

"Jay?" Claire's voice echoed in the small, tiled room.

My heart jumped and I couldn't stop the grin that spread across my face. Just hearing her speak made happiness pound through my body.

"Hey, beautiful. Do you need something?"

Please say me.

Maybe the other guys hadn't bothered to get her anything to eat? What was she doing in here?

"Um..."

She wasn't moving and she wasn't talking other than that first mumbled 'um'. I really didn't read women's minds, especially those I wasn't related to. I wanted desperately for her to want *me*, but for all I knew, she was about to ask for a ride home.

"If you give me a couple of minutes, I'll get out and help you."

With whatever it is you need.

"No! I actually.... um... could I join you, do you think?"

Could she join me? Hell, yes! "Of course, you can, but, ah..." How did I tell her that unless she wanted to get fucked again, she better stay away from me?

I didn't really get a chance to tell her anything of the sort.

She walked through the cloud of heat and moved toward me, joining me in the huge shower before I could even open my mouth and get out the words.

Naked. She was naked.

When had she gotten undressed? And why?

"Ah…" I didn't know where to look, without causing offence, but at the same time, I couldn't keep my greedy eyes off her beautiful curves.

Claire naked was even more delicious than I'd imagined.

She stood facing me and leaned back beneath the spray, wetting her hair and tipping her head back.

She lifted her arms to run her hands through her hair, her perfect breasts jutting up at me, the pink nipples erect and begging to be kissed.

I had about two seconds before I lost control, so I'd better get consent before my wolf took over.

"Claire, I don't know how to say this nicely, so I'm just gonna say it. I'm dying to mate with you and I'm afraid that if you don't leave this shower cubicle right now, I'm not going to have any chance of controlling myself with you."

Normally, this would be the furthest thing from the truth. I'd stopped myself at every level of sex with a woman, even after she'd come on me and I was balls deep inside of her. She'd asked me to stop, and I had.

That level of control was beyond me when it came to Claire, especially today, when I could scent my pack mates on her and her heat was causing a chemical reaction inside me.

"I don't want you to… fight that," she said. Her voice was husky in the steam. "I want you, too."

That was all she had to say and I was charging forward, picking her up and pushing her against the cool tiles.

"Oh my God. I need you, Jay. As much as the other two."

She bit into my shoulder and wrapped her legs around my waist.

I growled, deep in my chest, and supported her beneath the buttocks with my hands.

She needed me? Thank the gods for that!

I grabbed her ass more firmly, and lined her pussy up with my cock. I was so primed I had no hope of going slow today.

"Are you ready?" I managed, and she nodded quickly, clinging to my shoulders.

I tilted her pelvis with my hands and thrust up into her in one long, smooth movement.

"Oh my," she groaned out as her pussy swallowed me up and gripped me hard.

She was so wet, so aroused, and yet so tight. The perfect combination, and I growled as my shifter and human sides both recognized the rightness of our connection.

I had to squeeze my eyes shut and think of anything else but Claire, in order to gain some control.

I was going to blow right in that moment if I didn't.

What could I focus on? The cold floor beneath my feet... the tiles in the bathroom...

"Jay..." she whispered, and I was lost.

Nope. There was going to be no finesse today. No slow build.

This was going to be a hard, fast race to completion and possession.

I hoisted her further up the wall and her face lifted to look at me. I fastened my mouth to her lips, tasting her kiss as I began to ride her body.

I pumped into her hard and fast, slamming her into the wall and swallowing her moans as we kissed.

The water beat down on us and Claire broke off from our kiss to scream and cry out into the air.

"Yes. Yes. Yes, Jay! Harder!" she yelled, and I gave her all I could.

She began to come on me, her pussy rippling around my cock, tightening like a wound-up spring.

I was going to join her soon enough.

As she began to arch and stiffen, I thrust into her as deeply as I could, my balls hard against her ass as she started to orgasm.

Her pussy sucked on me like the perfect mouth, milking my cock and calling for my sperm.

I let all control go.

The heat that had tingled at the back of my legs erupted into a brush fire up my back and I allowed it to spread. My cock pulsed inside her, spouting my seed and giving her everything I had to give.

She shuddered in my arms, laying kisses on my neck and face.

I turned to her and kissed her deeply, slipping my tongue inside her mouth until the last of the tremors had stopped.

Then she pulled back and smiled up at me. "I can't believe how good that was."

I let her untangle her legs and slide to the floor.

She stumbled and I wrapped an arm around her, pulling her beneath the water and turning up the heat once again.

"Well, that was unexpected," I managed, and searched my body for any remnants of the raging testosterone that had been pumping in me all day.

She laughed and washed herself again and I couldn't stop a huge smile from spreading across my face.

It was gone.

The anger. The unsettled feeling I'd had driving my actions and busy activity around the house all day had disappeared. My shifter was happily curled up in a quiet corner deep inside me, sleeping the sleep of the satisfied.

This woman was indeed our mate, and it seemed that she had a magic pussy.

12

CLAIRE

I turned away from Jay to hide my hot cheeks and let the shower water course down over my shoulders and back.

What had I become?

I'd had sex with three different men in one day, when it had taken me a decade to sleep with three different men in the past.

What was happening to me?

I grabbed the soap and washed my body for the third time today, my breasts and the area between my legs tender, and my thighs trembling and sore.

"Thank you, beautiful." Jay turned me back to face him, and pressed another kiss to my lips. Then he stepped out of the shower, drying his magnificent body with a huge gray towel.

"Can I ask you a question? It'll probably sound strange," I queried, though a laugh trembled on my lips, a post-orgasm high making my head spin.

At this rate, I wouldn't be able to think after a day or two.

Perhaps that was their plan? To make me so weak with sexual satisfaction, I'd never be able to leave, because my brain would be mush and all I'd want would be more of this. More of them. All three of them.

I shook my head, filing the idea away to think about later, because at the moment, my body was telling me it might even be worth it to throw away my career.

I frowned, annoyed at where my thoughts were taking me. To throw away my career for the sake of sex, after twelve years of schooling that had led me into a profession that I loved, seemed ludicrous. And yet, hundred-hour work weeks and no sleep, versus being loved and cherished by three strong men... I almost let out one of those growls the guys threw around so easily. Why was I even thinking along those lines?

"Yeah, of course, ask me anything," Jay responded, wrapping the towel around his lean waist and looking at me expectantly.

Seriously, if I'd had a camera in my hand, I'd be click-clicking. Jay's eyes were dark and intense, his hair was wet and falling perfectly over his face.

And his body... *oh my God*. "How come you all have perfect bodies? Is that a wolf thing, or something else?"

Jay laughed and ran a hand through his hair, the movement making his abs ripple and his shoulder muscles flex. "Ah, yeah, kinda. We have extremely fast metabolisms, and we run a lot, of course. Not to mention the fact we're all tradies of some sort. Plumbers, electricians and builders. Physical jobs that keep us fit. We can pretty much do everything."

I stared at him and couldn't believe my eyes. Jay was the smallest of the three men, by far, and yet the strength behind his build was impressive.

After all, he'd just given me the hottest shower sex of my life, holding me up against the wall with ease.

No guy had ever been able to hold my weight for a few seconds, let alone for a vigorous session like that.

"Well, you're distracting me." I waved my hands at him. "I'll be down in a few minutes."

"Okay. I'll give you some time alone. But don't forget, dinner is downstairs when you're ready." Jay left with a soft smile on his face and I could finally breathe and think.

There was something pretty magical about these men, and it wasn't just the fact that they could turn into wolves. It was how I felt when I was around them.

Hornier than I'd ever been in my life, that was for damn sure.

Each time I went to bed with one of them today, I'd felt completely satisfied for several minutes afterwards, and then the ravenous hunger was back.

I searched my feelings and ran a hand between my thighs.

"Oh, thank God."

The insatiable need had subsided—finally.

It had grown all day, from the moment I woke up here in this strange house, and with each sexual encounter the pull had gotten stronger, to the point that I really had no idea how to satisfy the hunger in my body.

But now, it had settled. Calmed. I felt like I might actually be able to think now.

But why? Was it because I'd finally had sex with all three of them?

Was it possible that the strange mating connection thing they talked about might actually be true? Because I knew one thing. I wanted all of them. More than I'd ever wanted any one man before, I wanted all three of these guys, with a desire so strong I had never felt anything like it.

They were so different, so individually beautiful. And sexy... damn, were they sexy!

I'd convinced myself after my last failed relationship that the traditional path was *not* for me. There would be no doting husband, or multitude of babies for me. I'd have my work... my patients... my...

"Holy shit!"

I turned the water off and began scrubbing myself with a nearby towel.

Babies!

I hadn't even thought about contraception throughout the day. How crazy was that?

What sort of woman let three men come inside of her without a second thought?

A nymphomaniac for one, and a slut for another, said the shaming voice in my head.

"Oh, shut up."

I tried not to let the voice win and increase the panic that was already fluttering in my mind.

I counted on my fingers. My period had been two weeks ago, which meant I was probably on day sixteen of my cycle.

I should be fine. There was never a perfect science to conception, nor a completely safe time, but it *should* be okay.

I'd been on and off the pill for almost fifteen years now, though I wasn't on it at the moment. And the chance of ovulating at all after so many years of artificial hormones, let alone getting pregnant in one month at thirty-two, was... slim.

Not nil. Slim.

My medical brain was screaming at me about the repercussions of such rash actions, while my modern female brain chided me for being so reckless.

"Oh, fuck, off!" I practically yelled at myself in the mirror.

I'd never done a reckless thing in my life. Not once. I'd never taken drugs, never had a one-night stand, never taken a chance on anyone, or anything.

This was different.

I'd met werewolves, for goodness sakes! And then I'd bedded all three of them, in the very same day!

Surely some of the rules could be bent in this situation. Damn it, surely this one time I could even break the bloody rules.

I made my way back to Taylor's room and pulled on the jeans and tank I'd borrowed from Mary.

I was throwing all my pre-conceived ideas out the window. *Screw it.*

I had one more day with them, and I wasn't going to waste it worrying about whether I was doing the right thing or not by following my feelings.

Twenty-four hours until I had to go back to the city and start another fourteen-hour shift in an under-staffed hospital with a supervisor who hated me.

My heart ached at the idea of leaving, and with that strange thought came the realization of how much I was going to miss the three guys when I returned to my old life.

Which was crazy. I barely knew them.

But there was something there, between me and them.

They certainly believed I was meant to be here for them and I owed it to myself, and them, to see where this led. If for nothing more than scientific curiosity, although I knew this was so much more than anything scientific or logic-based.

I made my way down the stairs, noticing for the first time the wooden staircase and the carved details I'd missed when I passed this way last time.

Had they built this house?

All of it? How brilliant was that if they had.

There was general chatter going on in the kitchen, and as I made my way down and entered the room to find three smiling faces turning my way, my heart sang in recognition of a home I hadn't even known I needed.

"Ah, hi," I managed, my face flaming with heat.

Dexter got up off his stool and came toward me, sweeping me off my feet and twirling me around as though I weighed less than a child.

Which I could guarantee, I didn't.

I was a comfort eater, and it showed in my physique. Or so I'd thought, until I met these three men and they made me feel beautiful and valued, regardless of my weight.

"You hungry, gorgeous? You've barely eaten all day."

"Um…"

"Come, eat."

I had no idea how I felt… other than high on life. But I couldn't really answer that particular question without sounding a bit nuts.

I was ushered to the table to sit down to a plate of roasted lamb, crunchy salted potatoes, salad and fruit. My stomach began to gurgle at the sight of the delicious-looking food.

Maybe I was hungrier than I'd thought.

I began to eat and the men around me, who had already eaten, it seemed, fell into a natural conversation about work and the various people and activities going on in their lives.

I listened absently and looked around the kitchen, the space clean and well used.

Much nicer than my own apartment really, I thought, despite the feminine touches I'd added for color and warmth. After all, I was never home, so why bother keeping it nice all the time?

"So, what do you guys usually do after dinner?"

They all looked at me with sudden heat, the suggestive expression in Dexter's eyes in particular making me glance away. Okay. It was clear what they wanted to happen, after dinner. And by the curl of anticipation deep down in my belly, I suspected they might get their way. Again.

But that wasn't what I'd meant. "No," I clarified. "I mean, on a normal night."

"Depends," Taylor said, leaning over the table and grabbing a handful of berries. "Sometimes we just watch some TV, other times we go out for a run through the woods. We're up before dawn most days, so we go to bed pretty early compared to humans, I suspect."

I grinned at him. "And you know a lot about humans?"

He shrugged. "Not personally. But I guess just what we see on TV, or when we go into one of the cities, which is pretty rare."

Dexter moved across to me and ran a hand over my back. I looked up at him in query. "What would you like to do, beautiful? There's a pub of sorts nearby, where a lot of the guys hang out, play pool and drink. Would you like to meet more of the pack? Or..."

I shook my head. "Not at the moment. Maybe tomorrow."

The last thing I wanted to do was be around more of those intense stares, especially when there was alcohol involved, and my men would be outnumbered.

My men... what a concept.

"I'd love to see you all shift, if that's what you mean by going for a run."

I wondered if it would blow my mind, actually. Some part of me still didn't believe I was in a paranormal world, even though I'd had plenty of evidence of that, already.

I wanted to see it again. To verify that I hadn't been dreaming the first time.

Because if all of this were true, then the part of me that didn't believe in fated love or sex with multiple people might just be silenced forever.

The men looked at each other and I could see the fear in their eyes. Why were they afraid? Did they think they might accidently hurt me? I couldn't imagine such a scenario, not now that I'd connected with each of them physically, but then, I hadn't seen all of them in their wolf form. Maybe it changed something innate inside them?

"What's wrong?" I glanced between all three of them, waiting. Taylor was the one who eventually spoke up.

"Oh... ah..." He glanced at Jay and Dexter with an uncomfortable look on his face. "We're a bit concerned about how you're going to respond when you see us. We don't want to scare you off."

Oh. They weren't afraid of hurting me. They were afraid I wouldn't like them anymore. I wasn't sure how I was going to feel about it, either, but I could guarantee I wouldn't like them any less.

"Well, if you have a bottle of vodka, a couple of shots couldn't hurt."

"Ah..." That look again.

"Don't tell me you don't drink. Because I've seen beer in your fridge."

"Oh, we do." Taylor said. "Just not much hard liquor. With a pack full of unfulfilled, testosterone-fueled men, having an abundance of hard alcohol on hand isn't a smart move."

"I see." I winced at the thought. Yes, they were probably right.

"Well," I offered, "how about if Mary comes with me, or some of the other older women? Surely, they'll keep me calm, and make sure none of the guys drag me off." I laughed to show I was joking, but no one joined me.

I knew they were worried about the full male pack and, if I were honest, so was I. These young men had no women with whom to let off steam. It was a rather disconcerting concept, to say the least, and was one of the main reasons I had for not staying here, and wanting to return back home.

Eventually, Dexter nodded. "Mom may be the best plan," he said. "She's pretty relaxed with everything, and you two seemed to hit it off."

He sounded like he was talking to me in words, but I could see he was mostly speaking to himself, trying to reason out the best way to manage this.

Taylor nodded. "My mom wanted to meet Claire too, so how about I go pick her up and meet you guys back here?"

"Sounds like a plan." I clapped my hands and grinned at the guys.

I was high on life and sex and... sperm.

Ew.

God, it was good, though.

I'd never been able to orgasm during penetration, but with these men it seemed almost guaranteed. Their sperm alone seemed magical. I'd had a simultaneous orgasm with them every time.

Maybe that was also a sign that we were meant to be together?

"Hey..." I opened my mouth to ask something about the topic, and realized what I was about to do to myself. If I asked the question that hovered on the tip of my tongue, I was likely going to open a can of worms that I wasn't prepared for, and might lead to the green-eyed monster spewing forth.

Did I really want to know if they made all their lovers come during ejaculation?

I slammed my mouth shut.

No.

No, I did not want to know that.

"What, beautiful?" Jay asked as Dexter and Taylor headed out the front door to fetch their moms.

I thought quickly, trying to come up with an alternative. I couldn't ask the question I had planned to. Honestly, I just couldn't.

"Nothing. Just thinking about the wolf thing. You said you'll be in complete control, yeah?"

He nodded solemnly. "Yeah, always."

"Okay, then let me grab that sweater Mary loaned me and I'll be ready to go."

I stuffed a few more of the delicious berries into my mouth before I left the table.

Mary had let me borrow the softest black wool sweater, and as I pulled it on over my head and arms, I snuggled my face into it.

There was the sweetest smell attached to the wool. Whether it was the washing powder, or Mary herself, there was something that reminded me of Dexter in the scent. And that meant I wasn't taking off this sweater anytime soon. I loved the idea of being surrounded by my big, protective man.

Jay and I moved to the window together and he opened the front door for me, a sweet smile on his face.

"You look happy," I said to him.

He laughed and grabbed me around the waist, squeezing me tightly for a minute before letting me go.

"Of course, I am. I've got you. Life is perfect."

13

CLAIRE

For the first time since I'd had sex with them all, a tremor of unease ran through me.

I understood what Jay meant, of course. There was a huge part of me that felt the same way. I was happy here with them and knew I could continue to be, if I decided to take up their offer and stay.

If I never went back to my old life, things would be so simple.

But that wasn't me. I wasn't simple. I wasn't easily content. And a part of me knew I'd be fighting all three of them *when and if* I needed to go home tomorrow. The flicker of unease grew larger, but I managed to tamp it down, mostly. I would deal with that tomorrow. Tonight, I was going to witness magic. I was going to see all three of my men shift into another form.

"Looks like Dex is bringing the whole party here," Jay said, his tone dark.

What did that mean?

He grabbed my hand and we went through the front door, down the stairs and walked out onto the road in front of the house.

There was a large group of men and two older women walking

toward us. Dexter and Taylor were with them, but they both had grim looks on their faces.

I stepped closer to Jay and he slid his arm around me, holding me tight against his body.

"It's all right, Claire." Then he addressed Dexter. "What are you doing, Dex?" My men stepped out of the group to come closer to Jay and me. I counted six other men, besides my three.

Dexter was shaking his head. "Don't worry, I don't like it any more than you do."

Taylor and Dexter moved around to stand behind me and I relaxed again, feeling safe and warm now that my three men were surrounding me.

God, I could get used to this feeling. It was almost drug-like in its intensity.

Mary stepped closer too, smiling warmly. "Claire, some of the neighboring mini-packs wanted to meet you. I hope you don't mind."

Did I mind meeting six hunks with more muscles than I'd ever seen in my life?

Ah, no. Not really.

"Considering the lack of women in town, I can understand the interest," I murmured to Jay, and then I turned and addressed the strangers. "Hello, I'm Claire."

They all stared at me, but with none of the heat and lust I'd gotten used to seeing in my men's eyes. My tension reduced a notch.

One large man stepped forward, an Alpha I presumed by his bearing.

"I'm Grayson."

He didn't seem to want to come much closer, but I extended my hand anyway.

"An Alpha, I presume?"

He reached out with a sudden grin and I heard my men inhale sharply. Surely, I wasn't going to keel over if I touched this one, too?

"How'd you know?" he asked, and shook my hand in the same

way that had occurred a hundred times a day since becoming a doctor.

Nothing happened and I felt the pack at my back breathe a collective sigh of relief. My shoulders relaxed. I was still on my feet. No dizziness whatsoever.

"You're big," I said.

He glanced down in a sort of shy manner that surprised me. A gentle giant, perhaps? "It's nice to meet you, Claire. May I ask you a question?"

"Of course."

Damn, he had beautiful eyes, a nice manner and huge shoulders. And I could appreciate all that, yes, but there was no attraction. No want, need, or craving.

Perhaps I was fully satisfied? I turned to glance at Taylor over my shoulder, and my belly tightened. A smile lifted my lips. Nope. Still there.

I turned back to Grayson, who seemed to be weighing his words.

"Go on," I prompted. "Ask me whatever you want."

I was feeling relaxed and part drunk on sex. I'd tell them anything they wanted at this point in time.

"Can you give us a hint about what to look for with our mate, since it appears we all need to be on the hunt for a human now."

Ah. They wanted their own mates. Of course, they did. I was nothing to them beyond a source of information.

Some more of my internal fears relaxed. These men didn't want me, I just represented what they were looking for.

"Well, for one thing, I wouldn't use the word hunt when you're talking to a potential human mate." I grinned at him to let him know I was half-joking, and he smiled back. "But to be honest, I'm not sure what to tell you. Did Dexter mention the fainting thing?"

Grayson nodded. "Yes. But I was wondering if you had an idea before that. When you first saw them. Something I can look for in my mate, because I've met human women before and no one has ever fainted at my touch."

I assessed the big hunk and made some conclusions—fair or not, I wasn't sure. But I was about to find out.

"Maybe that's because your mate has a brain, like me, and you've been picking up tiny blondes with more boobs than anything else?"

A surprised grin stretched across Grayson's face, a cheeky light entering his eyes.

"They weren't all blonde."

Some of his pack mates laughed and then tension in the whole group began to ease.

"Look, I honestly don't know what to tell you. I'm a doctor who has barely dated in a decade. Maybe your mates are the same? Women who work too much and never get out, not to the places you'd usually go to find a date, anyway."

"Then how am I meant to find her?"

I couldn't believe I was going to say it, but there was no other answer.

"Fate. You have to trust that you'll stumble across her when the time is right. But I wouldn't be avoiding going to town during the day. If you guys can start going in more often, you'll have much a better chance of meeting the right one."

The men looked amongst themselves and nodded in agreement.

"That makes sense. Any other tips?" One of the other guys spoke up, and by his lesser size I'd guess he was one of the Omegas.

"Well, I will tell you that I knew there was something special about Dexter the moment I saw him," I said truthfully. "My heart was pounding and I could barely breathe. I've never had a response like that to any man before and I'm sure your mates will feel the same when they meet you."

They seemed happy enough with my answers, thanking me and heading off. Dexter pulled me into the circle of his arms and kissed the top of my head.

"Thanks for that, Claire."

"Oh, no problem. Happy to help." And I was. Why I was, I had no idea. I didn't belong here, and I certainly didn't know if I was going to stay.

But at the moment, I was going with the flow, and it had felt good to give those other guys hope.

"Let's go to the woods to watch them shift and run," Mary said, holding her hand out to me.

I pushed out of Dexter's embrace and linked arms with his mother, a small amount of fear suddenly weaving through my blood.

"Okay. Sure."

We walked around the back of their house toward what I assumed must be their shifting area. The whole town was cut into the woods in a natural way. Very little clearing had been done for the houses, and if these people were wolves who liked to run, I couldn't imagine a better location for their territory.

Another older woman walked up to us on my other side. She had long brown hair pulled into a ponytail, with streaks of gray lightening her temples.

"Hello Claire. I'm Sue, Taylor's mom." She introduced herself as we walked, shooting me a bright smile. I could see traces of Taylor's features in her face. I smiled back.

"Hi. It's nice to meet you."

We continued walking and my mind balked at the weirdness of the situation. If this was a traditional type of relationship, I'd have three mothers-in-law. How strange would that be?

"Have you seen any of them shift yet?" Sue asked as we settled to sit on a large wooden bench.

"Ah, yes. Jay sh...shifted." If that was the word for it. "He turned into a brown wolf right in the lounge room, which was pretty extraordinary... to put it simply."

Sue laughed. "Well, you're about to get a treat, because an Omega wolf is rather small and timid compared to mine and Mary's sons."

She indicated to the woods, where my three lovers stood about twenty feet away.

They stripped out of their shirts and began unbuttoning their jeans. Were they seriously going to get naked right in front of their moms?

Before I could look away, or voice my discomfort, the men were no more.

"Oh my God."

Instead, there were three huge wolves standing on the men's clothes, in varying sizes and colors.

I stood up, unable to sit. Unable to run away.

I took a few steps closer. I wanted to touch them. Something compelled me forward, as if I couldn't help myself. I stopped before I got too close, but I found that I wasn't afraid at all. I was enchanted by the sight before me.

"Dexter's the big silver one, isn't he?"

"Yes," said Sue from behind me. "And the black one is my Taylor."

They were magnificent as they began to jump and run and play around the trees of the forest.

"They're really beautiful."

And they were. Gone was my fear. In its place was awe and gratitude, and a burst of love.

Yes, *love*. Love for these amazing creatures and the world I'd been introduced into.

I watched my men—no, I corrected myself, my wolves—run for several minutes. There was a freedom in their movement that I couldn't take my eyes away from. I found myself grinning from ear to ear as I watched.

Then, out of the blue, there was a deep and unexpected growl that reverberated from the shadows in the woods, and all play among my wolves stopped. Instantly, they began racing toward me.

I staggered back and the mothers grabbed me.

"You need to get back inside the house. Now, Claire!" Mary's voice was urgent.

My wolves had run to me, only to turn and face the woods, ready to fend off whatever was coming.

Another growl sounded. What the hell was it? Another wolf? Something worse?

My heart began to pound with genuine fright. "Why? What's going on?" I asked breathlessly as Mary and Sue practically dragged me back to the house, up the stairs and in through the back door. My men were still out there. What were they facing?

Mary stared at me, her eyes wide with shock. "The bears are here."

Four words I never thought would accompany the terrifying sound of the ground shaking as what seemed like a dark and furious army charged toward the house.

14

———————

DEXTER

The ground shook with the bears' approach. I'd never seen so many in my life, and they were all charging toward us as one.

A wall of fur and fury. But I would not let them through. Not while my mate was in the house behind us.

Was that why they were here? To take my mate from me?

Never!

I bared my teeth and let out a vicious growl, then threw my head back and howled to the sky, calling for support.

We'd need help, and Grayson's crew shouldn't be far.

The bears broke through the woods line on all fours, running at full tilt.

I started toward them, growling and snapping as I assessed the best way to attack. The bears had more weight, but wolves were more agile. I leapt through the air and tore my teeth along the side of the Alpha bear's ribs and flank as I passed him.

He stumbled and fell, and I jumped onto his back, tearing at his throat as I attempted to roll him over.

He lifted a massive paw and swiped, pushing me down, hard. I swiveled, getting out from under his grip, and then jumped back onto all fours, snarling.

More bears ran past us and I wanted to scream in frustration. They were headed straight for my house!

I left the injured Alpha and raced after the bears that had broken away from us.

I reached the slowest one and sunk my teeth into its leg, trying to bring it down. As I did so, a pack of six wolves joined in the fray.

Grayson's pack, and Axel's too. Good. We were going to need them.

I tasted blood as I tore at the bear's flesh and it swiped at my face with a massive paw, tearing at my cheek.

I took a second to glance around, calculating. There had to be a dozen bears.

They'd never attacked us with such numbers before. Why now?

I could see Taylor and Jay out of the corner of my eye, working in unison to attack one of the bears.

It wasn't enough. We needed more reinforcements.

My mother's silver wolf bounded down the back steps of my house, growling and snapping at any bear that came close.

Fear whistled through me. They were trying to get into the house. They were here for Claire.

Should I get her out of the house, shift back to human and drive her to safety, drawing the bears away?

Or should we kill them all?

There were more wolves coming now, piling through the trees. We were outnumbering them two to one.

I raced over to my mother and stood in front of her, baring my teeth at any bears who made it to the stairs of our house.

This was my *home*. My *mate* was in there, and she needed to be protected, at all costs.

Why were they attacking? I needed to understand, but to do that,

I needed to shift back to human. Did I dare? I would be vulnerable if I did, but it seemed to be the only way to get them to explain this attack.

The bears and the wolves had been rivals for years, however nothing had ever come out of these useless fights.

I let go of my Alpha wolf, the shifter howling in anger as I released my strongest self.

I ran up the back steps and stood on my porch, naked and angry.

Some of the bears had begun to retreat but there were three still fighting, including the Alpha I'd taken down initially.

"What the fuck are you doing here?" I bellowed out, though my voice was strained and garbled from shifting. "Explain yourselves!"

The wolves fell back to line up with my house, guarding the town.

My pack stayed in wolf form, and rightly so. No one would be stupid enough to shift back, except me.

The Alpha bear began to transform. In his place stood a massive man, with a shaggy black beard and tattoos covering his upper body.

I walked down the two steps to the ground and glared at him across the grass. "What are you doing here?"

"We came to see your mate."

Taylor and Jay growled loudly from the line of wolves, their teeth glistening in the dusk light.

"Who the hell told you we'd found our mate?"

The man's eyebrows rose high. "*Our* mate? She's the mate to your whole pack... well isn't that interesting?"

His tone was nasty and I didn't like the way his eyes shone with malice when he spoke.

"You didn't answer my question," I spoke in a loud, commanding tone, so that everyone could hear our conversation.

"No. And I won't." He was equally commanding. Likely the leader of the whole bear pack. "You wolves should be extinct in a few more years and that's what Fate has decided. You cannot bring humans in for breeding. That is not our way."

"Our way?" I repeated. "We are nothing like you."

"You're more like us than you know, wolf."

The man shifted back, and the wolves of my pack crouched down, ready to fight again if necessary.

But the bears turned and left, moving like big, wounded elephants, through the woods and beyond, until they disappeared back into the shadows.

A couple of wolves followed, making sure the enemy really did leave our territory. I knew they would call us all in howls if they ran into difficulty.

Taylor and Jay began to shift back but I couldn't wait for them. I rushed inside to check on Claire.

Sue was with her in Jay's room, her arms around Claire's shaking form.

"Oh, sweetheart..." My heart broke to see her so scared.

"Dexter!" She leapt up and ran at me, throwing her arms around my neck, holding me like she'd never let me go. "Were they real bears? Or were they shifters too?"

"You didn't see the Alpha shift?" I drew her into the lounge and pulled her into my lap.

"No. I was with Sue."

Sue walked over to the door and my mother joined her, tugging her clothes back on.

"Dex, we're going to speak to the elders. Someone has to do something about this. It was a completely unprovoked attack."

I nodded and was glad when the women left.

"Do you know what they wanted, Dex?" Claire asked me, and I couldn't lie.

"They said they wanted you."

She had stopped shivering, and stood up to stare down at me. "But why?"

Taylor and Jay came in through the back door, dressed again, and threw me my jeans.

I quickly pulled them on.

"They didn't say why, exactly, just something about our pack being extinct in a few decades and that we're not meant to have mates, especially not human mates."

"You need to tell the elders," Taylor said, already heading toward the front door. He stopped when Claire began to speak.

"I need to get back to my apartment. Now. It isn't safe here," she said.

My poor love. The worry in her expression was very readable.

"Claire, you're okay. You're safe here, I promise," I said.

She looked at me with hurt in her eyes. "How can you say that, Dexter, after what just happened? They want *me*. What if they come back when you're not here?"

"We'll always be here. I'll make sure of it."

But I couldn't guarantee that, not really. Not the way the house was set up. We were the closest to the forest's edge.

And if I left Jay at home with Claire, how would he fend off a bear attack single handed? Even if we could get back here to help him, from wherever we were working at the time, it might be too late.

Impossible.

I turned to my pack. "I want to know how the hell the bears found out about Claire. She's only been here for a day."

"They have spies, obviously," Taylor said.

"Or surveillance cameras," Jay added.

I shrugged, and then shook my head. What were we going to do?

Claire was trembling again, and her face was red. She was obviously full of emotion, and looked ready to burst into tears.

I walked over to her and put my arms around her. "Claire. Everything is all right. You're safe."

She was shaking her head. "No. I want to go home. Now. Jay said you'd take me home if I asked, and I want to go home. Now."

What were my choices? I needed to attend to the threat to our pack, but my mate needed me, too.

Taylor stepped up next to me and laid a hand on my arm. My Beta. My best friend.

"I'll go to the council for you, Dex, although I'm sure the elders'll want to speak to you tomorrow. You look after Claire."

And there was the answer, in the strength and numbers of a pack. We all stepped up for one another, when we needed it.

"Thanks, Taylor." I shot him a warm look, letting him know without words how much I appreciated him. "Let them know I'll come over to discuss strategies in the morning. For now, I'll take Claire to bed."

Taylor left as Claire began to mumble. "No, I don't want to go to bed. I..."

I took both of her hands in mine. "Look at me, beautiful."

She wouldn't initially, but eventually she pulled her gaze up to meet mine.

"I know you're probably in shock, and want to run away, but right now it's dark, and it's dangerous to drive these roads when you're not in the right head space to do so. The bears won't come back tonight, and if they do, we have three packs next door who will jump at the chance to protect us."

Claire was nodding but I wasn't sure how much she was hearing.

"So, let's get you into bed and get some sleep, and tomorrow, if you still want to go home, I'll drive you back there myself."

It hurt to say it, but what other choice did I have?

"Do you promise?" Her voice was a whisper.

"Yes, darlin', I promise."

I'd never keep Claire here against her free will, and if she was the one the bears were after to stop us from breeding and continuing our pack, then perhaps she was safer in the city.

They'd never find her among the constant crowds at the hospital.

"Okay," she said quietly.

I picked her up into my arms. "I'm going to put you in my bed and we'll all join you to keep you warm and safe tonight, okay?"

I looked over at Jay, who nodded with a relieved look. We'd slept together on camping trips and when we were in our wolf form.

And considering we were about to spend the rest of our lives sharing a mate, if Claire agreed to stay, we might have to look at a redesign of the house. We could knock through one of the walls upstairs and create a huge bedroom with one massive bed, so Claire could be surrounded by all of us.

Or she might want us separately, but for some reason, I didn't see that happening.

Only time would tell, of course.

"Let's go, beautiful."

I carried her to my room.

The smell of our earlier sex still lingered, but it was the darkness and warmth I knew she craved now.

We stripped off our clothes and climbed into the king bed. Claire lay in the middle, and Jay joined us. He and I cocooned Claire, one on either side of her.

I lay awake for hours, listening to the sound of Claire's breathing, feeling her soft skin against mine, and hearing the regular breaths of Jay nearby. It was remarkably comforting to lie like this.

Taylor came home sometime around midnight and, when he poked his head in, I gestured for him to join us. He quickly undressed and settled into the other side of the bed next to Jay, his fear and worry a tangible presence in the room.

Eventually I heard Taylor's breathing change too, as he fell asleep.

We didn't speak until the morning, but for me, my whole world changed that night.

My life no longer revolved only around my pack.

My world had expanded to include Claire. Her safety, her love, and the health of my individual pack mates were all now my priority.

If we needed to move, to live somewhere else, become new people with new identities, I'd do it.

I'd do anything for the woman whom Fate had deemed the perfect person for me, for Taylor, and for Jay.

She'd carry our babies and love us forever, I was sure of it.

She was the only constant, the only thing I could count on now. Maybe she didn't know it yet, and maybe we'd have to beg her to stay after the fear the bears had instilled in her, but we'd work it out.

We all would.

Because no one was getting between my pack and our fated mate.

15

CLAIRE

I was wrapped in warmth and love and protection, like a pillow and dreams and chocolate.

My stomach grumbled. Hmmm... chocolate... damn I was hungry.

I was also sweating.

I opened my eyes slowly, my body enjoying the feeling of being in the bed with Dexter, and... I opened my eyes. Jay lay beside me.

I lifted my head and looked over his shoulder. Taylor had joined us as well.

All three of them were fast asleep in bed with me, and I felt... complete, for the first time ever.

Happy.

Whole.

God!

I rolled my eyes at my own stupidity. My own feminine fairy tale gone wrong.

I'd never wanted to be a woman who defined herself by the man in her life, or in this case, the *men*.

But here I was, for the first time in my whole life, feeling truly happy. My mind began to clear, allowing through the feelings of love that had been complicated by the fear of last night.

In the light of day, my fear of the bears had lifted, though not entirely disappeared.

In its wake was more confusion and questions than anything else. And a need to make sure the wolves were not simply a smaller version of the bears.

I had to go home, where I could have the time and space to think clearly and make some important decisions about what I wanted in life.

And if they let me go, then that would prove to me they cared.

If they didn't... then I wasn't sure what I was going to do. I couldn't be with three men who held me against my will, and yet, I couldn't imagine not being with them.

I almost groaned aloud, and shifted impatiently at my own recalcitrant thoughts.

"Good morning, beautiful." Dexter's voice rolled over my head and I looked up to see him smiling down at me. He must have felt my movement, and it woke him.

"Good morning."

My stomach gurgled again, and I was suddenly very aware of being naked and surrounded by three naked men. Three very sexy, naked men.

"Ah... breakfast time?" Jay smiled sleepily at me, too, and I nodded.

Taylor stood up first, his tight body drawing my gaze, as did his semi-erect cock.

Morning glory... three of them.

My cheeks heated, and my belly fluttered. If I had time... boy, would that would keep me busy!

"What are you in the mood for?" Taylor asked. "Pancakes? Bacon and eggs? More sex, perhaps?"

I giggled as I slid off the bed and away from the temptation that was my triad.

They could so easily drag me into another full day of sex. One-on-one, or three-on-one, I wouldn't care.

When there were no set limits, the list of things that I could do was astronomical.

"Maybe later." I smiled at Taylor. "Some pancakes first would be amazing."

Jay stood up, his body just as beautiful and aroused as Taylor's. God, these men were gorgeous. "They're my specialty. I'll start mixing up some batter."

I watched him leave, enjoying his tight ass flexing as he walked. I sighed.

I lived alone. No one had cooked me breakfast in years, if I didn't count the Starbucks down the street. The barista who worked there often made me coffee and handed me a fresh muffin.

But to have a man who cooked? Completely independent men who could do everything for themselves? What a dream. Every married friend of mine would be jealous once they found out.

Found out what? That I had three boyfriends, all of a sudden? How was I going to explain that?

A cold shudder flowed over my skin at the thought of the disgust, the fear, and the misunderstanding that would surround me for the rest of my life if I accepted this way of life for myself.

"Um. Thanks, I'd love that. I might throw some clothes on. They're downstairs, I think."

I fled the room before I sank to my knees for the men. I could feel the need growing in my belly, the heat between my thighs flaring. But I had to be smart about this. I needed a clear head.

I raced down the stairs, my breasts bobbing up and down and still tender from yesterday's attention.

I held them with both hands and snuck over to where I'd left clothes last night on the couch.

Mary had loaned me a dress, so I pulled that on, not bothering with underwear. I wasn't going to wear what I'd had on yesterday, and I wasn't borrowing any.

Wearing one of your lover's mother's clothes was a little strange as it was.

"Pancakes coming right up!" Jay announced, as he bounced down the stairs wearing only a pair of faded jeans. At least one erection was neatly tucked away. For now.

I bit my lip to stifle the moan as one after another, the guys came down the stairs and stepped into the kitchen.

They were like a well-oiled machine, getting out ingredients, plates, drinks and fruit.

I hung back and watched, my mind instantly thinking about how well they'd work on me if given half a chance.

I barely stifled the giggle that rose at the thought and Dexter turned to stare at me with his sexy eyes.

"What shall we do today, beautiful?"

Ah. This was where it was about to get tricky.

"Don't you guys have work today?"

Dexter grinned. "Yeah, tons. But that can wait."

"Um..." I had to say it. I took a deep breath and blurted it out. "I'd like to go home after breakfast, please."

All three men stopped stirring, pouring and generally moving, to turn around and face me. Three matching sets of shocked eyes stared at me.

Dexter cleared his throat. "Claire... I know the bears scared you last night, but you don't need to leave straight away."

"Yes. I do. I need to get home. Make sure they haven't put out a missing persons' report on me. Little River is only an hour away. You said you'd take me home today, if I asked."

And that was the cruncher for me. They'd promised.

I had to know I had a choice to be here with these men. We'd started this bizarre relationship with them pretty much kidnapping me. It couldn't continue to be so one-sided.

"True... I just didn't think you'd want to go home so soon. We could spend the day together..."

Dexter's tone was suggestive and despite my stomach quivering at the idea of what would happen if I stayed, I put up both my hands and metaphorically pulled my big-girl panties on.

So to speak.

"No. I have a job and a life to get back to, not to mention your father, who I'd like to check up on. So please, after breakfast I'd like you all to take me back. Come see my apartment, my life. If we're going to make a go of this... relationship, you have to accept parts of my life, too."

It couldn't all be one way. They couldn't just move me into their home and forget the rest of my life existed.

It wasn't fair, and I deserved choices.

The three men all looked at each other, confusion plain on their faces.

Eventually Jay spoke. "Okay, Claire. We'll come back with you. Let's just finish eating breakfast, and then we'll leave."

They were letting me go? Something deep inside me let go and I began to relax. I'd won this round, and I could put some distance between us so I could think.

Which was impossible when I was around these guys.

They were too sexy, too sweet, too intoxicating.

So, we ate pancakes and then bundled into the truck and headed back to the city. Back to my life.

The drive was awkward, and despite Jay chattering away, trying to break the tension, no one seemed to know what to talk about.

When we hit the city outskirts, I began directing them to my apartment.

"Left here, and then you can park in front of the apartment block. It's the tall one just over there."

I'd bought a place only a few streets over from the hospital a few years ago, since my whole world revolved around work.

"Just here. Great. Do you want to come up and see my place?" I asked them, and they all looked at me like I'd asked them to cut off my hand.

"Is there an elevator, or stairs?" Taylor asked.

I had to laugh a little at his expression of concern, equally obvious on all their faces. "There are stairs, but we'd take the elevator to mine. You don't have to. I can just go change and come back, and we can go to the hospital, if you'd prefer."

"I'll come," Jay said, popping out of the back seat and opening the door for me.

Taylor and Dexter stayed firmly in the car. "We'll wait for you. No problem."

I turned away to hide my smile. These men had taken on bears set on ripping them apart, and not shown any fear. The idea of climbing into an elevator and entering a human apartment? I could see how much the idea alarmed them.

"Let's go, Jay."

The smallest, the Omega, and he was the one willing to brave the terrifying elevator ride? I grinned at Jay as he walked next to me, not so close as to touch me, but like my shadow, moving as I did.

We went into the building, up the elevator and along the corridor to my sixth-floor apartment.

"You okay?" I asked him.

Jay nodded, swallowing hard. "Yeah. I'm not used to being this far off the ground. Feels weird."

I shrugged. "I don't even think about it, really. It was the best I could afford when I was a resident. I paid it off and haven't really looked for anything better since. I'm barely at home anyway, to be honest."

I kept a spare key in a lock box at the end of the hall and as I grabbed it, my stomach tightened with unease.

What was I doing back here? At my old apartment that I never really liked anyway?

Oh, stop it. Now you're just being silly.

I palmed the key and walked over to my apartment. *Number three.*

The irony of that made me smile as I opened the door.

Jay walked in behind me and whistled as he looked around. "Nice."

I tried to see my sterile living space the way he did. As a flashy new piece of technology with all the mod cons.

"Yeah, thanks. Let me change and we can go."

I went straight to my bedroom and pulled out a pair of black slacks and a long, gray sweater.

Comfortable, covered and professional. Always, unless I couldn't help it.

I reached for my old, comfortable cotton knickers and hesitated. If the guys came back to my place tonight... no.

My hand hovered over the lace.

Yes. I grabbed my nicest bra and panties—the only matching set I owned.

They'd love it, I was sure. If they got the chance to see it, that is.

I rushed back out and found Jay in the same spot I'd left him.

"Wow, you look great," he said.

I smiled in thanks. I didn't feel that great. Nor that comfortable back here, actually. I thought I'd be relieved to be back home, with all my familiar things. But the trip back here was more disappointing than I'd expected.

Then again, considering I did little more than sleep in my apartment, I shouldn't be that surprised.

It was the hospital that was my true home.

"Let's go see Dexter's dad."

Jay nodded and down we went once again, not seeing a single soul I knew. Jay seemed relieved to be back on ground level once again, and I patted his arm to show him I appreciated his effort to accompany me upstairs.

I was anxious to see Jack Monaghan, not only from a doctor's perspective, but also from a personal one. What would Dexter's dad be like?

"They should have operated last night, so we should be able to see him in recovery today," I said, as we drove the few blocks to the hospital.

"Park in the underground car park. I've got a staff card."

Dexter pulled in and I swiped my card so we wouldn't have to pay for parking.

The light went green and we went into the familiar concrete cage.

When we got out, all three men were stiff and uncomfortable.

"What's up?" I asked, leading the way to the elevators.

"This place is terrible," Dexter said, looking around at the concrete walls and dark spaces.

"Yeah, I suppose it is." I'd never really thought about it, except from a safety aspect, which was typical for women.

It was daylight, so for me it was much less scary than at any other time. Walking into the carpark alone at three a.m. wasn't fun.

"Let's go see your dad."

We made our way up to the surgical ward and I located Gerry, the surgeon who'd worked on Jack last night.

"Where'd you go yesterday, Claire? No one saw you leave and some of the nurses said they saw a big guy carry you out of Emergency."

"Um... yeah. I wasn't feeling well yesterday, Gerry. Tummy bug." I waved vaguely in my stomach region. "Sorry I didn't stick around to do hand-over properly."

He shrugged, although I could tell he wasn't impressed by my lack of professionalism in running off mid-shift.

I opened my mouth to apologize again, but decided against it and shut up. I strived to be an exemplary employee. I was never late, often did doubles, accepted extras, and was always on call.

Unlike Gerry, I didn't have a wife, or kids, or golf. So, for the one time I didn't do everything right, which was not even my choice, I wasn't apologizing again.

"Tell me what happened with Jack Monaghan."

Gerry launched into a post-op round of information and I took the chart from him to study the entries while he spoke.

"He handled the operation better than any surgery I've ever done. He's bouncing back like he never had a problem in the first place."

I smiled gently and tried not to roll my eyes. So, they hadn't picked up the fact that Jack was a werewolf.... Correction—wolf shifter.

Good.

His bloodwork looked normal, too, which surprised me. Obviously, if there was a marker for the paranormal side of these shifters, it didn't show up on routine checks. Or perhaps, humans just didn't know what to look for. Relief filled me. For some reason, I felt protective of the life the pack had built for themselves, alongside the human world but not quite of it.

"Great. I'll pop in before my shift to check on him. Thanks, Gerry."

I turned and left the surgeon, who was giving me looks like I had no right to speak to his patient.

I did. And I would.

I made my way around to Jack's room in the surgical ward without telling the guys, who were waiting for me out front. I wanted to meet Jack by myself, for some strange reason.

With butterflies fluttering in my gut, I knocked on the glass window and made my way into the room.

"Hello, Jack, I'm Doctor Claire. I was here when you were admitted yesterday."

Jack's gaze came up and my breath tightened in my chest. They were Dexter's eyes. Same cool blue. Same calm, steady confidence.

"Hello, Claire. When can I go home? And where is my family?"

I laughed, pulled up a chair next to him and sat down.

"You certainly get straight to the point, don't you, Jack?"

"I know what's important, and that's getting out of here and going home."

I smiled and picked up his wrist, counting his steady heartbeats with my fingers. His color was good, with no blue in the fingertips.

I stood up and checked his hour-by-hour chart. "This all looks great. When you came in yesterday, I wasn't even sure you'd survive the surgery, let alone be practically ready to go home the next day."

His eyes lit up and a smile curved his full lips. "I can go home today?"

"Soon."

I walked back around the table, wanting to stay close to him for some reason. The pull of an Alpha male, perhaps?

"Hey, Claire..."

"Yes, Jack?"

"Why do you smell like my son?"

I glanced toward the other bed in the ward. The other patient was asleep, and intubated. Probably not capable of hearing or understanding what I was about to say.

"Um... because yesterday after he dropped you off, your son kidnapped me and took me home with him."

I tried to say it with the same calm and professional manner that I reserved for my patients, but I lost the battle when heat flushed up my face.

Jack's eyes went wide and he studied me with more interest. "He took you back to the pack?"

I nodded. "Yes, and I met Mary and Sue, and Grayson, and Jay and Taylor, of course."

"But why would he..." Jack was looking confused, until his gaze snapped together sharply and he stared hard at me. "You're his mate, aren't you?"

He looked me up and down like he was assessing my size, weight and strength.

I grinned at him and nodded. "Not just Dexter, but Taylor and Jay's, too," I said softly.

His mouth dropped open. "But... you're human," he said. "And... three of them? A whole mini-pack?"

I laughed out loud at his shock. "Ah, yeah... on both fronts. Human, and all three of them."

"But that would mean..."

"That we humans are going to save your pack, Jack."

He sat up straighter in bed, his naked chest catching my attention. The strength and size of him at sixty years old would rival his son. And the huge scar now bisecting his ribcage only added to the image of toughness.

"You've mated with him? With *them*? You're going to stay?"

"Oh... ah..."

Shit! Why had I said I was going to save them?

Did I want to stay with the pack? I had no idea at this point, but surely we could work something out.

After all, the hospital was only an hour away from where they lived.

"We're working on a compromise. But for now, I'll go get them if you'd like? They're here in the hospital."

"Mary, too?"

For the first time I saw a softness in the Alpha's eyes and it touched my heart to know the depth of love he still felt for his mate after all these years.

"No, just Dexter and the boys. But I'm sure we can get your wife in soon."

A nurse bustled in, checking vitals and being a general annoyance, if the look on Jack's face was to be believed.

"I'll bring your son in to see you in a few minutes, Mr. Monaghan."

I winked at him as he rolled his eyes.

And I went and found my wolf triad.

16

DEXTER

I looked up from the uncomfortable hospital chair. Claire was waving at us to come over to her.

"Let's go," I said to Taylor and Jay.

We stood up and followed our mate through the sterile hospital, until I finally saw my father, alive and well. He was sitting up in bed with a smile on his face like I'd never seen before.

"Dex!"

I leaned down and put my arms awkwardly around my dad, holding him tight. I hadn't realized how much I'd missed him until now. I didn't want to let him go.

"Good to see you, Dad."

I pulled back and the nurse excused herself from the room.

Claire pulled the curtains around us and we all squashed into the small space.

My father looked at me with an expression I couldn't read. "You've found your mate."

Surprise pushed through me and I looked from Claire to my father.

"Claire told you?"

"I could smell you on her... and not just you." Dad's gaze went from Jay to Taylor and back to me.

He suddenly looked slightly less impressed.

"Yes. Claire is our mate—my pack's mate. She's bonded to all three of us."

"So I understand. But, how is that possible?"

Claire giggled and shook her head, putting her hand on her forehead. "You tell me, Jack. I think we'd all love to know the answer to that question."

Dad looked around the circle and we all began to smile. He'd missed so much and he'd been gone only a day.

"When I met Claire yesterday, I knew she was my mate as soon as I saw her, and then she fainted the moment I touched her."

Claire rolled her eyes and my father's mouth dropped open. "Really? Well, that's a new one."

"It happened again when I shook her hand," Taylor piped up.

"And sort of with me, but she didn't quite pass out," Jay said, his smile showing how proud he was to have Claire as his mate, too.

My dad fell back against the pillows, his eyes wide with wonder. "Well, I'll be damned. It's actually true."

I laughed. "Yeah, it looks like we do have mates, Dad, but they're not from our pack."

"And we all thought it was the end," my father said, almost to himself.

Claire stood up and began opening the curtain. "I have to check in before my shift tonight, but you guys stay for a bit, if you want. I left my phone and everything in my locker yesterday, so my parents probably think I'm dead."

She headed off with a smile and I sat down into the chair she'd vacated.

"It's been a pretty full on twenty-four hours, Dad."

"I can imagine."

Taylor leaned against the wall with a beeping machine mounted upon it. "Yeah, and with the bears attacking last night, we're not sure what to do with Claire now."

"What?" My dad sat bolt upright, then winced and put a hand to his scarred chest.

"Relax, Dad. No one was hurt, except a couple of the bears."

But they'd heal like we had, and wouldn't be feeling it by next week.

"Why would they attack?"

I shrugged and leaned back in the chair. "They said it was to get Claire, though I don't know what they were going to do with her if we'd have let them in the house. Kidnap her? Kill her?"

I shuddered as prickles of unease worked their way up my spine.

"But how did they even know about her?" Dad asked.

Taylor grunted. "We either have a spy in our mix, or they're watching us and put two and two together. Claire is only the start. Once the other packs begin finding their mates, we'll have a proper town again. Children. Full of life and laughter and love. We'll be stronger than ever and the bears aren't going to like that."

We talked for a while, but eventually I could see that my father was getting tired.

"We'll come back later, Dad. I'll bring Mom in, if you want?"

"Yes. I'd like that."

The nurse returned and started making annoyed noises and looking at us as though we weren't meant to be there.

"We're going. Don't worry."

"He needs to rest," she said, checking his suture wounds and tapping at the IV attached to his arm.

"Thanks for looking after him," I said, giving her a smile.

She softened and gave me half a smile back.

And then we left to find Claire.

"What are we going to do about our mate, boys?"

I could tell Claire was unclear about her path and the last thing I wanted to do was force her into a decision that would ripple poison through our future.

Taylor stared at me. "I want to take her home again. But, I guess we can't do that, unless she wants it."

I laughed. "Life would be simple if we could just lock her in the bedroom so she can never leave. But no. We can't."

Because, boy did I want to do that as much as I could sense Taylor wanted it. My wolf was in total agreement with that plan. But we had to be smarter than that.

"But... we can't," Jay said quietly.

"No," Taylor said, and I nodded my agreement. It had to be Claire's choice, now, as to how our future would play out. We had to trust that the connection she felt with us was as strong as what the three of us felt, for her.

We made our way out of the hospital and into the sunshine. I breathed in and gratefully inhaled the fresh air. Damn, it was stuffy in there.

"We need to give her a choice, whether we live here in the city or go back to the pack. But I won't let her go, not for anything," I said gruffly.

Taylor nodded and Jay grinned. "Agreed."

So now we just had to tell our gorgeous doctor that.

"Let's go find her."

We went back into the hospital with our heads held high, gave the nurse in charge a message for Claire, and sat back to wait.

I'd do anything for my mate. Even get a job in this filthy city to stay close to her, if it came to that. It probably wouldn't be too bad... but I had one condition.

I wasn't living in that massive building with those dog-box apartments.

I'd build her a house, as close to the hospital as possible. A ground-level house, with all the mod-cons she wished for.

And my mate could have everything. Her job *and* us.

If she still wanted it all.

17

CLAIRE

"Doctor Masterson, there's a patient in the E.R. wanting to speak to you." The nurse had been passing my desk and stopped.

"Me? Oh, who is it?"

I'd just finished answering the hundreds of texts, emails, Facebook notifications and messages on my phone.

Now, back to my men.

"He wouldn't tell me, but he's very agitated and asked for you by name and description. I can tell him you've left for the day, if you want?"

I wanted to go back to Dexter, Taylor and Jay, but what if this was a shifter who needed my help? Grayson, or one of his pack? Had one of them been injured in the fight last night?

"That's okay. Which bed is he in?"

I couldn't text Dexter or Taylor, which was going to be a problem long-term. Cell phones for all three of them were going to be a necessity, especially if I kept working the hours I already did.

The nurse told me where to find the patient. I walked into the

E.R. and grabbed a clipboard. But when I pulled back the cubicle curtain, a shriek caught in my throat.

This man was a shifter, I was sure of it. But he wasn't a wolf. From the shaggy hair and beard, and the heavy build, I could tell he was more likely a bear.

"You!" he growled as soon as he saw me, lunging for me with both hands out.

I ducked his attack and ran straight to the wall that held the emergency alarm. I pulled on the red lever as hard as I could and a siren shrieked through the main floor.

He grabbed my arm and threw me across the room. Pain splintered through my elbow as I knocked into a metal trolley and rolled across the floor.

People started screaming and running through the E.R.

A security guard attempted to stop the bear, and the big, bearded man threw the guard into a glass cabinet as if he were a small toy.

Oh, fuck.

I hugged my elbow, pain radiating everywhere. There was a surgical tray above me and I used it to stagger to my feet. I grabbed a scalpel from the tray, the only weapon I could see that might be of use.

"Come at me again and find out why I got top marks in all my anatomy classes," I managed to growl at him, baring my teeth for emphasis.

I may not win this fight, but I knew where all the main arteries were, and I could make him bleed.

He charged at me, ignoring my threat, and I ducked beneath his outstretched arms and hit the floor, slicing out with my knife and cutting across his big gut.

He had jeans on, which made his legs harder to get to, but if I was quick, I might get him next time.

The bear howled and grabbed for his stomach.

Now my ankle was killing me in addition to my elbow, but I focused on the man, searching for weak points.

The wrists, the jugular, the femoral artery.

I had to get him before he got me, and as my heart pounded with the ferocity of a steam engine, I knew I was in trouble. I was too small for this.

He put his arms wide out and began thundering toward me once again.

I heard a deep growl in the background but didn't turn to look as I gripped the scalpel and prepared myself for the impact to come.

Dexter rushed past me and knocked into the bear like one truck against another.

The impact was enough to shatter bone.

Taylor and Jay were on him too, punching and wrestling and thumping him until the bear stumbled toward the exit. My men rushed out after him.

I dropped the scalpel, and trembled like a leaf. "Holy hell," I muttered, unable to believe what had just happened.

More security guards ran by and followed the man outside. But they'd be too late, I was sure. The bear would run. He'd have to.

My legs weren't going to hold me much longer, so I staggered to a nearby seat and managed to land on the plastic rather than the floor.

One of the nurses rushed over. "Are you okay, Doctor?"

"Ah, yeah. I think so."

My ankle was throbbing and my left arm was hanging by my side at a weird angle. But the arm had mostly stopped hurting.

Hmmm... adrenaline's a wonderful thing.

"Let's get you admitted."

I stood up as Taylor came barreling back into the E.R.

"Claire! Claire." He came straight over and grabbed me. Pain screamed through my body and I yelled out.

"Oh, fuck. Are you okay?"

"I... yeah. But I think I broke something."

Taylor backed up a step, his face a mess of concern. "Oh, God, I'm sorry." He stepped forward again, and gingerly cupped my cheek for a moment. The warmth gave me a tiny burst of strength. I smiled at him, and then a wheelchair was pushed at me and I fell into it. "I need an x-ray, and some pain meds, I think."

I let the nurse wheel me away and left Taylor in the E.R. to wait for Dex and Jay.

I tapped the nurse with my good hand. "Can you make sure the guys find me later on? They'll be pestering you, I'm sure."

"Who are the guys?" she asked.

I couldn't help my smile. "*My* guys. Dexter, Taylor and Jay. You'll know them when you see them, trust me."

I'D BEEN MORE accurate than I realized. My men made the nurses' lives hell for the next few days as I was patched up, medicated and told to rest. My ankle was merely sprained, but the arm had indeed been broken, in two places. It would heal, eventually, but for now was a damn nuisance.

They wanted to visit constantly, and between Jack and myself, one of them was on the hospital grounds at all times.

"And don't worry, we have Grayson's pack guarding the hospital too, in shifts," Dexter told me a few days later as I packed my bag to go home.

"That's a bit of overkill, don't you think?"

My Alpha had been wracked with guilt for days over my injuries and I'd barely been able to calm him.

All three of them had been nothing but doting since the incident, and it was beginning to wear on me.

"Not at all," he said as he puffed out his chest.

"Hey, Claire, I have your final blood test results, and you might want to check this out."

Toma, one of the interns, handed me the sheet with a smile, her eyes flicking over to the massive Alpha standing by the window.

And then she left.

"What does she mean by that? Is something wrong?"

"No... I don't think.... *Oh...*"

I stared down at the results in my hand.

I was pregnant.

Already? How is that possible?

I folded the piece of paper and tucked it into the back pocket of my jeans. That was a conversation for later.

I wasn't even ready to think about it myself yet.

"What's wrong?" Dex asked.

"Nothing," I lied. "My iron's low, so I'll grab some supplements on the way out."

That wasn't entirely a lie. I did need iron supplements now. And folate too. And maybe a whole range of amino acids if I was growing one—or more—babies, inside of me.

What did wolf shifters have anyway? One at a time? I had no idea.

Dexter grabbed my bag and we walked to Jack's room, where he, too, was being packed up to go home.

"I cannot wait to get out of here!" he declared.

Mary smiled and kissed her big man, who was on his feet and looking strong.

"We can't wait to have you home," she said. Then Mary turned to me with that calm expression that never faltered. "Are you coming home with us, Claire, or staying in town tonight?"

My options were laid out in front of me, and the guys had made that crystal clear too. I could live anywhere, as long as they were allowed to go along for the ride.

And despite the stress and danger of the bears, I wouldn't have it any other way.

"I've been put on sick leave for four weeks with my arm, so I may as well come home with you for a bit."

I caught Dexter's eye and he grinned, but no one said anything more. It was like they were afraid to break the spell in case I changed my mind.

Jack and I signed all the release forms, and when we walked out the front of the hospital, I got a nice surprise.

"What are you guys doing here?"

Jay and Taylor leaned against a new four-by-four, with a bull bar, roll cage and more. "And what's with the new ride?"

Taylor threw Dexter the keys and he held them out to me. "We got it for you."

"You bought me a car?" Well, a truck was more like it.

I blinked at them, unable to believe they were really handing over such an expensive gift.

My own parents made me buy my own dinner on my birthday, and my men were just handing over a brand-new, monster-sized truck?

"Of course! We want you to be safe when you're driving. This thing'll run over a bear if you happen to come across one," Taylor said with a wink.

Jack and Mary walked up. "Nice truck! We'll see you at home."

I moved closer to my new truck, awestruck by the sheer size and shiny paint. "Um... I don't know what to say."

Jay opened the passenger side door. "Say thank you and jump in."

I grinned and resisted the urge to kiss his beautiful lips. "Thank you, guys. It's great. *Really* great."

I got in, with a little help from Jay, given my one-armed effort didn't quite work, and we headed back to the pack. I left the window open and took lots of breaths of clean air as we followed Mary's car.

My men and I hadn't had much time alone in the past few days, and I could feel the need for them growing in my belly.

"It'll be great to get home. I've missed a proper bed."

Among other things.

"We think you'll like what we've done. We've rearranged Dexter's bedroom so we can fit two king size beds in there now, side by side," Taylor said from the back seat.

I swiveled around to grin at him.

"You guys moving in to one bedroom, huh?"

Jay rolled his eyes. "Only if you're there. I'm not sleeping with them on the nights you're at the hospital."

I laughed, the happy sound filling me up and making me settle into the huge bucket seat and fully relax. "Well... I look forward to seeing it when we get home."

Home. That word meant something, when I considered where we were headed. A smile lifted my lips.

There was nothing but comfortable silence in the truck for a while, then Dexter cleared his throat.

"Um, we were wondering if you'd prefer to live closer to town, Claire? We've got money, and skills that are hireable. We could get a plot of land, and build a huge house for you."

I glanced across at him.

They loved their pack, and their home. "Why would you do that?"

I looked back at Jay and Taylor, who were glancing at each other nervously.

"Because we love you," Jay said, quietly, as though scared to voice such a thing.

Warmth filtered through my chest and made stupid tears spring to my eyes.

"But why would you leave the pack? It's your home."

Taylor sat forward on his seat. "Because you're our future. Our family. We'll do anything to make you happy. Go wherever you want to go. Well, anything but live in that tiny apartment of yours. That's where we draw the line," he said with a gorgeous grin.

Once again, I didn't know what to say.

"I love that you want to make life easy for us, and I love that you're willing to compromise, but so am I. I can drop some shifts at the hospital, and only stay in the apartment when necessary," I said.

I saw Taylor's brows come down and smiled at him. "Or we can buy a house on the outskirts of town and all be there most of the time, together. I don't care. An hour's drive is really nothing."

My proclamation was met with broad grins and Dexter's hand slid across my thigh in a possessive move.

"There's been no sign of the bear shifters since the hospital. In fact, when Grayson's pack went to investigate their known dens, they seem to have moved on," Dexter said.

"That's great."

I was relieved to know that the men who seemed to want me killed were gone for now.

Some people... seriously. They just didn't want anyone else to be happy.

"How are you feeling today?"

A shiver raced straight through my tummy at Dexter's question.

"Why? You wanting to show me the new bed?"

Dexter shot me a grin. "Yep."

I turned back around to face the road and settled into my seat.

"Sounds like a plan."

We were home before I knew it, and the sun sparkled bright, happy light all over our house.

Talk about a homecoming.

The guys all jumped out, and Taylor opened my door and scooped me up like I weighed nothing at all, although he was very cautious of my injured arm.

I didn't bother complaining, I just clung to his neck and hoped he didn't drop me.

He went straight inside and up the stairs, into what used to be Dexter's room.

All furniture had been removed except for one massive bed filling half the room, wall to wall.

"Whoa." They hadn't been joking. We could fit a whole football team on this bed. Or four big, strong shifter men, and their woman. My tummy wobbled in anticipation.

Taylor put me down gently and I flexed my fingers inside my cast. I had to be a little careful of the arm, but everything else was working just fine.

"Looks good, doesn't it?" Dexter asked as he walked up behind me, his massive chest vibrating with his words.

I leaned back against him, loving the feel of him. His strength, his size, his warmth.

"I have no idea how I'm going to explain you guys to my family or my friends."

Dexter chuckled and wrapped his arms around my waist. "Tell them Taylor's your boyfriend and we're his cousins, friends, whatever."

I twisted around in Dexter's arms and looked up into his heated gaze.

"Why Taylor?"

"Yeah, why me?" Taylor asked, as he stepped up to the bed.

"Because he's the most socially acceptable. I'm too big, Jay's too nice. Go with Taylor."

I laughed and lifted my head up for a kiss. "I doubt they'll believe me, when they see how we all are with each other. But we'll work it out."

And we would. I knew we would. I was home with my men, and I certainly wasn't worrying about semantics now.

Dexter ducked his head and kissed me, his lips tasting of need and pure male.

Salty and sweet and so delicious I bit into his bottom lip with my teeth.

Yum.

I tugged at his shirt, wanting to feel his skin, but struggling with one hand.

"Can you strip? I can't with this stupid arm."

There was a deep chuckle that sounded from all three men simultaneously and within a few moments, I had all of them naked before me.

Three men, three hearts, three cocks.

And they were all *mine.*

Happiness pulsed through me as I pushed at my clothes and Jay stepped forward to help me, getting me out of my dress and underwear like a pro.

And then they were on me, kissing me, touching me, lighting my body on fire.

All three of them.

Just as I had imagined, over and over, ever since the day I mated with them all.

Dexter lay me down on the bed and knelt on the floor between my legs, while the other two lay beside me.

He grinned at me with that devilish smile, kissed my thighs and stroked my belly with his hands.

Jay, my sweet one, licked my breasts, sucking at the sensitive tips and making my nipples ache.

I moaned and gasped and searched for Taylor, who met my lips with his, stifling my groans and making me drink kisses from his mouth.

Dexter lifted my legs so that my feet rested on his shoulders, opened me right up, and ate my pussy. Licking my core's juices and suckling my clit until I was screaming.

He didn't stop, pushing me higher and higher while Jay's teeth tugged at my nipples. My pussy exploded in an orgasm so sweet it brought tears to my eyes.

I shuddered and shook, my belly convulsing with the pleasure they'd brought me.

Dexter stood up and grinned down at me, his cock thick and hard in front of him.

I had to taste it.

I sat up and bobbed my head down, sucking the tip into my mouth and groaning at the exquisite taste of him.

Then Jay and Taylor knelt on either side of me and I was turning my head to suck one and then the other in turn.

None of them needed the foreplay—they were all hard and ready for me, but I loved the teasing. Pleasuring them. Drawing out the moment until they took me.

When my arm was better, we could take our time—one day, when the need wasn't so great.

For the moment though, I was aching, my belly tight and desperate for them.

I sucked Dexter one more time and then looked up at him.

"How are we going to do this?"

The men moved into position, as though they'd been planning this.

"You're going to take all of us," Taylor told me as Dexter lay on his back on the bed.

"At once?" I asked, swallowing nervously.

Jay nodded.

I needed to go with it. Fate had gotten me this far, so there was no point being afraid now.

"Okay."

"Come here, beautiful," Dexter called, and I climbed on top of him, loving the feel of his huge, hot body between my thighs.

"Take me inside you," he demanded, and I lifted up. The feeling of Dexter holding his cock against my entrance made a squeal of excitement rise in my throat.

I can't wait.

I slid down on his shaft slowly, loving every inch of him stretching me, filling me up.

"Oh, God... that's so good."

Taylor's hand pushed at my back and I leaned forward, resting my good hand on the bed.

Taylor's fingers ran something cold and wet over my ass and Dexter began to thrust up into me, distracting me from what was about to happen.

"I'm not sure..." I hadn't done that before.

"Trust us," Dexter said, playing with my nipples while his cock pumped gently inside me.

Taylor slid a single finger inside my ass and I gasped out against the burning pain.

"Relax, if you can," Taylor urged, and I concentrated on all the other sensations in my body. The pulse of my pussy tightening around Dexter, the pleasure in my nipples.

Then the burn began to fade, replaced by a strange emptiness, a hunger. He stretched me until I was moaning from the pressure.

Taylor withdrew his finger and I gasped out, pushing back toward the pressure again. Needing it.

But then his cock was sliding into me and I had to force myself to breathe, the pain overcoming the pleasure. He was so big!

And then there were vibrations. A small clit vibe was being held to me by Jay, who grinned at me.

"Let go, Claire. We've got you."

I closed my eyes and let the feelings consume me.

Neither man was moving, and I needed them to do something.

"Move. Please."

Taylor slid out and slid back in, and Dexter grabbed the vibe and began pumping up and down with his hips.

"Oh. My." The pleasure in my core amplified to the extreme.

I couldn't think, couldn't breathe. Could only feel.

And then Jay pressed his cock to my lips and I opened for him.

The moment his taste slid across my tongue, I came.

I cried out as my whole body tightened and spasmed around them, rejoicing in the joining of all three parts of me.

Dexter groaned and began thrusting faster. Taylor did too, jerkily moving in and out.

"Oh, fuck, I'm gonna blow!" Taylor yelled out.

I sucked hard on Jay's cock, not wanting him to miss out.

Jay thrust his hips in time with my other mates, all three of my holes full and aching for release.

Taylor was first, filling me with his seed and pushing heat into my body.

"Oh, fuck!" Dexter cried out and Taylor pulled out, leaving Dexter to pound into me, faster and faster.

My pussy was tightening again and I let go of Jay's cock. "Please, fuck my ass, Jay."

I couldn't believe the words were coming from my lips, but I was empty and wanting him back there.

Jay jumped down the bed and stood behind me, sliding straight into my body and crying out with me as we were once again joined.

Jay stayed still, pulsing inside of me as Dexter thrust so hard he moved all three of us.

"I'm gonna come," Dexter groaned, grabbing my hips with rough hands.

Jay grabbed my waist and began thrusting fast and hard.

The waves of pleasure picked me up and tightened me, cutting off my air, my thoughts, everything but the feelings between my thighs.

I heard Dexter cry out first, and his seed began to pulse inside of me. Then Jay followed him.

I couldn't hold on anymore.

I screamed, digging my nails into the mattress as I came so hard I saw stars.

Jay filled me from behind and my body shuddered and shook until I collapsed onto my mate's chest.

I was finally connected wholly to my entire pack.

Jay slid out of me, but I stayed on top of Dexter, wanting one of them inside of me. I'd feel far too empty without him.

Jay and Taylor fell onto the bed beside us, their gasps and groans of satisfaction filling the room.

"I cannot believe how hot that was. I can't even explain it." Dexter was stroking my back and chuckling with happiness.

"Best day of my life, by far," Jay was saying, and I looked up with a dopey smile, almost incoherent.

But I had to say it.

They had to know.

"I think I can make this day even better."

Dexter pulled a pillow down for himself and tucked it beneath his head. He ran a hand over my cheek.

"Oh, really? How?"

I smiled up at them all, their full attention on me.

"I'm pregnant."

EPILOGUE

DEXTER

One year later.

~

It had just gone sunrise and the packs were gathering in the meeting area.

The area was so much cleaner now, thanks to the mates who had completed our families.

I didn't stare at broken beer bottles and dirt any longer, with the scent of testosterone choking me.

The packs were settled, happy, and flourishing.

"Claire's still sleeping, so I thought I'd let her rest." Taylor handed me one of our twins, a boy, born three months ago.

Another wolf for the pack.

"Hello, my son, did you give your mother hell all night again?"

My babe gave me a sleepy smile and nestled into my arm, where I held him tight.

"They both did, didn't you hear them?" Taylor scowled at me and I shrugged. I usually slept through most of their crying.

"You're the most demanding, aren't you, beautiful girl?" Taylor held our daughter up in the air, and a sigh of true contentment stole my breath.

The first daughter born to our pack in over fifty years.

A true miracle—just like her mother.

I looked back over the yard. The grass was tended, the tables and chairs arranged in an orderly manner.

The women had brought so much with them when they moved in. Not just happiness, love and sex for three frustrated men.

But they had also brought with them the need to prosper and grow. To protect and nurture, as we were designed to do. Our mates had truly made us whole.

"She's perfect," I declared.

Jay groaned as he walked out of the house rubbing his eyes. "That's because you don't spend half the night walking her up and down the hallways."

I grinned and took my daughter in my other arm, loving the feel of our children nestled against me.

"You wanna go back to the way it was last year?" I asked them both, already knowing the answer.

That despite all their belly-aching, they loved our new family.

"What, with no Claire? No kids? No, thank you," Taylor declared.

Jay shook his head. "Hell no."

I laughed and watched as the other packs began to rise and my mother walked toward me with her arms stretched out for her grand-children.

I handed my daughter over to her and kept my son tight against me.

All of these changes were thanks to my mate.

Her strength, her kindness, and Fate.

Fate had shown me the way to our mate, and in the process, we had healed our whole pack.

THE END

PROLOGUE

GRAYSON

I could smell the fear rising from the woman in front of me. The scent made me want to back away, to save her from the discomfort.

But this wasn't about me, this was about my pack. My family.

I *needed* to speak to this human mate that Dexter's pack had found. *Claire.*

Dex had said I could ask some questions of Claire if I kept my distance. It was an odd request but I was willing to honor it, if it meant I might get some answers.

What was Dex worried about? I wasn't going to hurt her. He knew me better than that.

Or I thought he did.

Because if he was worried about me trying to steal Claire away from him, that was laughable. The last thing I'd do was try to take something that didn't belong to me. That wasn't my style at all.

Not that Claire the doctor wasn't pretty. She was. But I couldn't sense the animal magnetism that Dex and his pack mates, Taylor and Jay, boasted about.

To me, she didn't smell sexy. Instead, she smelled like... *theirs.*

And my Alpha wolf didn't stir for any taken woman. Especially not one already mated to another. Or in Claire's case, with three fated mates.

Claire stepped closer to Dex's Omega, Jay, who grabbed Claire and hauled her against his body in an uncharacteristically alpha-like gesture.

I turned my face away, to try and avoid them seeing my disbelief. It was all I could do not to laugh out loud. What did Jay think I was going to do? Grab their mate, strip her down and take her in full view of everyone here?

"What are you doing, Dex?" Jay demanded, and Dexter stepped away from our group to stand by his mate once again. Dex's Beta, Taylor, quickly joined him. Claire was flanked by her three pack mates, all of them vibrating with tension.

Dexter shook his head. "Don't worry, I don't like this any more than you do."

Seriously? What was wrong with these guys? Their human mate *could not possibly* be that precious.

Taylor and Dexter flagged Claire, with Jay moving slightly behind, and she relaxed into them, a soft smile lighting up her face.

That smile, and the comfortable familiarity between them all, was the first sign I'd seen of a true connection between her and her mates, and it was reassuring to see. I hadn't really been sure it was real, until now. Their connection was what I wanted... what I craved. A mate. A true love. Someone who would feel like the missing part of me. Someone I would die for, if I had to.

Mary, Dexter's mom, stepped up to speak to Claire for us. She'd brokered the discussion with Dexter, raising the issue we wanted answers to, and it was due to Mary's influence that Dex had agreed— albeit reluctantly—to let us meet his mate.

"Claire, some of the neighboring packs wanted to meet you," Mary said. "I hope you don't mind?"

Claire looked us up and down from the safety of her mens' arms, and said, "Considering the lack of women in this town, I can understand the interest." She looked straight at me this time. "Hi, I'm Claire."

I was the one who needed to step up and talk on behalf of the others, obviously. "I'm Grayson."

Claire extended her hand. "An Alpha, I presume?" she asked with a raise of one delicately arched eyebrow.

I grinned in acknowledgment and heard Dex inhale sharply. What was he worried about?

"How'd you know?" I reached out and shook her hand.

After a couple of seconds of what felt like tense silence, there was a collective sigh of relief from Dex, then Taylor and Jay.

Claire shrugged and withdrew her hand. "You're big."

I fought the heat that flashed up my face and glanced down at the huge body my Alpha genes guaranteed. "Ah... you're learning our ways, I see. It's nice to meet you, Claire. May I ask you a question?"

"Of course."

I opened my mouth, and then shut it again, hesitating instead of plunging forward. How did I ask her what we needed to know? She represented a solution to our problem, but it was a solution none of us had considered, until now.

For fifty years, not a single female had been born to our pack. The elders had believed that it meant our fated mates were non-existent for our generation. A romantic myth that had ended with our parents' matings. And in that assumption, the inevitable decline of our pack had been at the forefront of everyone's minds.

But Dexter had found his mate in the human population. And even more unusual, he'd found one female for his whole pack of three wolves. Claire had turned out to be the fated mate of Dex, Taylor *and* Jay, and she was one hundred percent human.

Was that really the future for the other mini-packs of three men, including mine? To share a woman in such a way?

"Go on, ask me whatever you want," Claire repeated.

I sighed and just went with what was in my head. "Can you give us a hint about what to look for with our mate? Since it appears we all need to be on the hunt for a human now."

Claire tilted her head. "Well, for one thing, I wouldn't use the word *hunt* when you're talking to her." She grinned at me and I couldn't help grinning back.

This one had a cheeky streak. Dex and his pack would need to stay on their toes.

Claire continued. "To be honest, though, I'm not sure what to say. Did Dexter tell you about the fainting thing?"

He had... and I suddenly realized why they'd been so hesitant to have me touch her. They'd been waiting to see if Claire keeled over when we shook hands.

But we hadn't. Interesting. That meant she really was fated for Dex's triad of wolves.

"Yes," I said, after a moment. "But I was wondering if you had an idea before that? When you first saw them, maybe? I need something that I can look for in my mate, because I've met human women before and no one has ever fainted at my touch..."

Claire looked me up and down like I was a piece of meat in a butcher's case, assessing me in two seconds and somehow coming up trumps. "Maybe that's because your mate has a brain, like me, and you've been picking up tiny blondes with more boobs than anything else?"

A grin stretched across my face. I couldn't help it. So, what if I liked them easy? We only had one night each visit in town to get them into bed, and then we had to kick them straight back out again.

There was no point trying to pick up any of the decent chicks. We literally didn't have the time, nor the desire before now, to connect with humans in a long-term manner.

I was unable to resist rising to her bait. "They weren't all blonde."

My Beta, Aaron, laughed beside me, and the tension in the whole group began to relax.

Claire shrugged. "Look, I honestly don't know what to tell you. I'm a doctor who's barely dated in a decade. Maybe your mates are the same? Women who work too much and never get out—not to the places you'd usually go to find a date, anyway."

Why didn't she just ask me to find a needle in a haystack?

"Then how am I meant to find her?"

Claire bit her lip and glanced away. Then she looked back at me with a reluctant smile.

"Fate," she said. "You have to trust that you'll stumble across her when the time is right. But I wouldn't be avoiding trips to town during the day. If you guys can start going in more often, you'll have a much better chance of meeting the right one."

I looked over at my Beta and he nodded.

"Any other tips?" Brad, my Omega, asked.

Claire looked to Brad. "Well, I will tell you that I knew there was something special about Dexter the moment I saw him. My heart was pounding and I could barely breathe. I've never had a response like that to any man before and I'm sure your mates will feel the same way when they meet you."

A sense of relief filled me at her words. There was hope. I had to focus on that element. Hope that there was a mate for me. For *us*.

I just had to ignore the surprisingly massive mountain of doubt and worry that threatened to bury the hope.

I leaned forward and got her attention, my mind spinning with the implications of what she was saying. I needed to get a job in town. At the very least, it would bring in more money for my pack, and best-case scenario... I'd actually find our fated mate.

"Thank you, Claire."

Dex pulled her into his arms and I took that as the signal to move off.

"Thanks Mary." I nodded at Dexter's mom and gestured to my mini-pack—my Omega and Beta. "Let's go."

Fifteen years ago, the elders of our pack passed a new law. Due to the lack of females and over-abundance of male shifters in our pack, we were told to arrange ourselves in triads. We had to form our own mini-packs, with an Alpha, a Beta and an Omega to each family.

I hadn't known Aaron or Brad very well when they'd approached me to become their Alpha in a pack, but it had worked out better than we'd expected.

I'd die to save them, every day of the week. They were my family. But I also wanted my mate, and if that meant sharing her with Brad and Aaron, as Dexter had done with his pack, then I would.

Anything to have a true family, and maybe even children one day.

I hoped our mate—if she existed—would one day fulfil the aching need inside my chest that I'd had for more than a decade.

I loved the larger pack, the elders and my blood-related family. But there was a place inside my heart that was gaping wide open. Empty. Ready and waiting for a woman to love and cherish.

"So, what do you want to do?" Aaron asked me as we walked to our front door and stepped inside our too-large home.

"We need to go into town and cover as much ground as possible. I'll apply for a job and see what happens. Our mate has to be out there."

"A job? Where? On a building site full of men?" Aaron rolled his eyes and I stopped to consider his words.

He was right. We were tradies. How were we going to meet women that way?

"There're women at employment agencies. You could apply for jobs everywhere and not necessarily take any," Brad piped up, and I turned to smile at him.

My Omega was quiet, but smart as a whip.

"That's an idea. Somewhere to start, at least." I glanced at my watch. It was only one p.m. There was still plenty of daylight left, to begin the process of looking.

"I'll go and ask some of the elders if they need anything from town. Might hunt around a little now."

"I'll go with you," Aaron said, his mouth setting with determination.

Brad shrugged. "I've got work to do here. Let me know how you go."

Aaron and I headed to the elders, but it seemed they needed nothing today. Then we jumped in the car and drove to town, a strange vibration of excitement rattling through me. I could tell from the way Aaron held himself, that he was feeling the same kind of strung-out anticipation, too.

When we arrived in Little River, I looked around with fresh eyes.

The air was cleaner, crisper and better than it had been the last time I'd been there. The colors were brighter and the sounds around me happier.

I knew it must be all in my imagination, but how could I not be feeling more positive after the chat with Claire? There was a chance that we could meet our mate, and soon.

"Should we split up and try different places?" Aaron asked, clearly struggling to hide his own smile.

Women walked by us, their gazes skimming over our bodies and some of them sending subtle invitations with their eyes.

I knew that humans were attracted to us. They liked muscles, of which we had an abundance.

It didn't mean much in the pack. Everyone was strong, hard-working and super-fit.

But in this world, where people worked while sitting in a chair all day, the men were not as strong, healthy, or trim.

"Yeah, why not," I said in answer to Aaron's query. "We could walk around, and see if anyone faints at our feet." I grinned at Aaron and he laughed.

The hunt was on.

I glanced around at a pair of women walking up the street, their long, straight hair billowing around their faces, their too-skinny legs wrapped in thin skirts.

I inhaled deeply, hoping to smell something new, sweet, and distinct.

But there was nothing except the normal scents of the city. The people around us offered up a range of scents, but none grabbed my attention and held it.

I went to turn away, but Aaron grabbed my arm. "Do you think we'll have a different mate each? Or one to share like Dex's pack?"

I shrugged. "No idea. Doesn't really matter, either way, does it?"

"Guess not." He sounded a little uncertain. Then he added, "You don't care?"

I stared at him, surprised by his question. "Of course, not. After spending a decade coming to terms with our shitty, one-night-stand existence, I'll do anything to find my true mate. To have a woman to come home to, and children. If she's meant for you and Brad too, then so be it."

I didn't have jealousy issues like a lot of the other Alphas.

I lived for my pack.

And if Fate had decided one human was enough for us, then I would ride that wave and be grateful for it.

"Oh, good." Aaron seemed happier now, more relaxed. "I feel the same way."

We grinned at each other, and I could read the hope in Aaron's eyes, now.

"Let's go," I said. "See you back here in two hours."

He grunted and we turned in opposite directions.

I walked along the streets and ducked into a pharmacy, a green grocer and a liquor store, making small talk with the locals, telling them I was looking for some work in housing construction.

None of the women smelled any different to me, and I shook so many hands. Everyone's hands.

They must have thought I was the politest person around.

And yet, no one fainted at my touch. Not even an offer to go out for dinner or a drink.

Not that I should have expected to find my mate on the first day. That would have been ridiculous. But as the time dragged on, my heart grew heavy. And when the designated time came and went, I forced myself back to the car, to discover Aaron's sad face.

"No luck?" I asked him, though the question was barely necessary. His slumped shoulders and the defeated set to his jaw made the answer too apparent.

"No. Although I inquired at a job recruitment agency and they said they'd call in regards to an interview... or something like that. I wasn't really listening, to be honest."

We got in the car and I turned the key. I was surprised by the amount of disappointment running through my blood. It felt like a cancer, insidious and potent.

I forced out a laugh, trying to lighten the mood. "After a decade of thinking we had no fated mate, we shouldn't expect her to just turn up on our doorstep in the first hour, right?"

Aaron nodded, then stared out the window and didn't say anything else.

Mopey bastard.

I sighed and turned the car back toward the pack.

Despite my conscious efforts to stay positive and grateful, Aaron's shitty attitude pretty much summed up how I felt, too.

We'd waited long enough.

I didn't want to wait any longer.

It was our time to find our mate. To begin our life. To finally be a true family. Because, without a woman or children, we were nothing.

CONTINUE READING: HERE